GRIZZLY BAIT

Falling down onto all fours, the bear walked toward McComb until it was barely eight feet away. Keeping his eyes on the huge animal, McComb reached slowly for his big Bowie. As he drew it from its fringed sheath, the blade glinted in the morning sun.

The bear raked at the dirt with its forepaw and threw gravel onto McComb. He saw it was ready to charge and got on one knee, the knife ready for use.

"Okay, if a showdown's what you want," the mountain man grunted, "then you damn well got one."

Almost before the words were out, the grizzly attacked.

The bear knocked him down, grabbing his body with both its powerful forelegs and trying to bite his neck. Moving quickly, McComb shoved the blade of his knife into its thick chest and pulled upward. It snarled in pain, but kept on fighting. McComb withdrew the Bowie and stabbed deeper. Dark blood covered both man and beast.

Suddenly, the animal stopped, then released its iron grip. Coughing, it moved off McComb, turned briefly then fell heavily onto its side, its back leg kicking the man in the gut one last time before it died.

SCALE TO THE HEIGHTS OF ADVENTURE WITH

MOUNTAIN JACK PIKE

By JOSEPH MEEK

MOUNTAIN MAN'S FURY

Ralph Hayes

PINNACLE BOOKS
WINDSOR PUBLISHING CORP.

Chapter One

Emmett Skinner waited in the dark.

A half grin creased his ugly, beefy face as he heard the rustling sound in the corner of the urine-odorous cell, like the sound of a quill pen on paper. Lying on his side on the lower bunk, Skinner also heard the measured snoring of Wylie above him. Sleeping had always seemed like a waste of time to Skinner. He had never been able to put more than two or three hours of it together at a time. Not since those early days when he had had to lie awake until his drunken father had returned home, to see whether he would bust into Skinner's room and begin beating on him again. Anyway, there was hell to be raised out there, when a man was free from prison bars, and Skinner had always preferred hell-raising to sleeping. Now, in this lice-infested hellhole, he could only think about all he would do when he got out. And when he thought about it, it was always McComb that sprang into his head as a first priority, like a fever he could not break.

The rustling sound was repeated. Skinner's hard,

piglike eyes turned toward the drain in the floor, and he saw the shadowy form there. The rat was back.

Skinner's thick left hand grasped a six-inch length of wire tightly, a piece he had bent off a bunk spring. It was straight now, and he had ground a point onto one end by scraping it on the concrete floor. It protruded from his fist about three inches.

The rat was big and fat because it had access to small amounts of garbage from several cells. It came warily across the floor, toward the bunks and the dried chunk of bread that Skinner had placed on the floor there. Skinner stopped breathing. The rat hesitated, then came on. Four feet away, then three.

Skinner's arm swung down in a swift, deadly arc, and the wire stabbed into and through the surprised rat, impaling it on the metal.

There was a lot of squealing and squirming. Skinner sat up on the bunk grinning, swinging his feet to the floor, holding the moving rat out in front of him.

"Got you, you little son of a bitch!"

The snoring above Skinner ended in a snort, and Wylie sat up, looking around in consternation. "What the hell!" he muttered.

Skinner stood up and held the dying rat in Wylie's face. "I told you I'd catch the thieving little bastard! Here, want an early breakfast, Wylie?" He thrust the rat up close to Wylie's lean face.

Wylie backed away. "Damn, you're making me

sick, Mule. Throw the goddamn thing down." He shoved a pair of glasses on his nose.

Everybody called Skinner by the nickname, because of his body strength, and his mental rigidity. With Wylie watching in disgust, Skinner stuck the head of the rat into his mouth, and bit it off cleanly, then spat it onto the floor. He unskewered the body then, letting it also drop to the floor. He still held the stiff length of wire in his meaty hand.

"Oh, Christ!" Wylie gritted out, making a face. He was a rather, skinny, flesh-wasted man with greasy hair who got along well with Skinner simply because he accepted Skinner's absolute domination of him in their enforced relationship.

Skinner wiped at a smear of blood at the corner of his mouth, and spat again. "This ought to do the job, Wylie my boy." He showed Wylie the skewer of wire. "Your part is to make me a wood handle for it, so I can drive it in easy."

Wylie nodded, sleep in his eyes. "I can handle that. Now let's get some sleep. It's hours yet till dawn."

Skinner ignored him and leaned on the upper bunk, looking past him. Skinner was a big, bulky, muscular man with a bald head, thick neck, and tiny, black eyes set deeply in facial muscle. His nose had been broken and flattened in some long-ago brawl, and his full mouth usually was held in a cruel, twisted shape.

When Skinner had been very young, a swaggering brute of a father had ruined him for good. His mother lost to the influenza before the age of five,

Skinner had had to live in a small cabin with a man who showed him no affection, and beat him regularly. "You got to be tough to make it out there," his father would tell him, as he approached puberty. The beatings ordinarily came when the older Skinner was drunk, and would strike without warning or reason. In better moods, his father would sometimes roughhouse with him, and even these supposedly friendly episodes could turn unexpectedly violent on his father's part. The fact was, his father enjoyed hurting and humiliating him, and for Skinner there was no escape from it. So at the age of fifteen, Skinner murdered his father by chopping his head off while he lay in a drunken stupor.

"It was just like butchering a hog," he would later confide to drinking partners, with a too-bright glitter in his eye.

His father had created a monster.

"I'm doing it tomorrow night," Skinner said now, still staring past Wylie. Wylie glanced at him, his head back on his pillow. "I'm busting out of this dung heap."

Wylie sighed. Nobody had broken out of Devil's Hole Prison for several years, and the present warden had sworn that nobody would again. "Sure, Mule," Wylie said, removing his glasses again.

"That supply wagon's been coming in later and later," Skinner said. He rested his chin on heavy forearms. "It's due tomorrow, and it will get here about dusk, and leave after dark."

Wylie turned his head toward him. "You got yourself on the supply detail?"

8

Skinner grinned derisively. "You got clabber for brains, four eyes. There's guards watching the supply detail, when they're unloading. I'm hauling garbage out of the mess hall tomorrow night. Nobody goes that fifty yards with me. And I'll end up within ten feet of that supply wagon, just about when it's getting set to head out. I'll wait till the supply detail is gone, with their guards, and then I'll sneak onboard that wagon. I'll be gone before the mess hall guards miss me."

Wylie absorbed all of that. It sounded surprisingly workable. Skinner did not look smart, but he could be. What he was, Wylie thought, was cunning. Wylie would not want him as an enemy.

"Sounds like it could work," he offered.

"Oh, it'll work," Skinner said in a low, rather hoarse voice. "I'll be gone by two more sunups." He stared some more. "I heard my old partner Lazlo is back in high pass country, to the west. I might just look him up."

"That's the Gypsy drifter you talked about?" Wylie said, stifling a yawn. Skinner had mentioned a band of renegade Gypsies he had met up with, a family of outlaws who traded trinkets to the Apaches and Shoshonis, stole from white men, and occasionally killed for profit. They had emigrated west from Ohio.

"That's him," Skinner said. "Him and me, we worked pretty good together." It had been on a rampage with Yuray Lazlo that they had gone into the cabin of a mountain man named McComb, murdered McComb's friend, and kidnapped his

Apache woman. McComb had later tracked him down and turned him in to the law, and Skinner had then been convicted and sent to this place of incarceration.

"Him and me might just get together again," Skinner said. "But first, I got me this priority thing to get out of the way."

"What would that be?" Wylie said.

Skinner replied in a growl. "I'm going to find me that goddamn mountain man that tracked me down and put me in here. That stinking, lice-ridden, Indian-loving son of a bitch that took it on hisself to cause me trouble. I'll see that motherless bastard in hell with his back broke, I'll cut him up in little pieces when I get my hands on him. He'll die slower than if the Blackfeet made a ritual killing for him, by Jesus."

Wylie licked suddenly dry lips, and looked away from Skinner's hard, evil, little eyes, and the thing he saw in them. "I hope you find him, Mule," he offered somberly.

"You just get me that handle for my pick," Skinner said ominously. "You just get it, Wylie. Today."

Wylie nodded, and felt a pinprick of sweat pop out on his upper lip. "Don't worry, Mule. I'll help you."

Emmett "Mule" Skinner grinned that twisted grin in the meaty face. "I never worry, Wylie," he said softly. "Never."

* * *

The following morning, Wylie turned a seven-inch handle for Skinner's weapon, on a steam lathe, augured a hole in its end to receive the thin metal rod Skinner had made, and then shoved a couple inches of the rod into the handle, gluing it in there. The final product looked like an ice pick. Wylie delivered it very surreptitiously to Skinner in the mess hall at the noon meal, ate his rancid-tasting soup and hardtack quickly, and obtained permission to leave the big room ahead of the others. He wanted to keep as far away from Skinner as possible, for the rest of that day, because of what Skinner had planned for the end of it. No sooner was Wylie gone, though, than another man came and sat down in his place beside Skinner. He was a thin, wiry fellow named Logan, and he had a desperate look on his bony face.

"I overheard you and Wylie talking earlier," he said in a sibilant half whisper.

Skinner looked over at him slowly, a dark scowl on his face. Across the table, other convicts were eating busily and noisily. A guard paced the aisle near them, carrying a shotgun.

Skinner stuck a last chunk of hardtack into his mouth.

"You're breaking out of here," the wiry fellow said. Skinner turned and gave him a deadly look. "I want to go with you."

Skinner chewed the bread. That goddamn loudmouth Wylie had caused him trouble. He chewed and said nothing.

"I got to get out," Logan said feverishly. "My

woman is sick. I got to see her before she's took off."

Skinner stared straight ahead. "Keep your god-damn voice down," he said almost inaudibly.

Logan looked around. The guard with the shot-gun eyed him momentarily, then walked on. "I'm serious about this, Skinner. If you won't include me in, I'll make trouble." His voice trailed off at the end, revealing fear and uncertainty.

Skinner slowly turned to him. The gray prison shirt he wore hugged his muscular shoulders tightly. His thick face subtly changed, became less harsh. "Maybe I can work you in, Logan. I'll meet you at the latrine at break time."

Logan met Skinner's hard eyes and nodded hopefully. "I'm much obliged, Skinner."

Skinner sat there another fifteen minutes without speaking again to Logan, then got up and left. The midday break was about over, and he returned to work in an area adjacent to the mess hall.

The afternoon passed slowly for Skinner. He found an excuse to go out to the carriageway where the wagons came in, and inspected the area for the last time. It should work, if he timed it right. He stared out through the open archway and into the prison yard, then beyond it to a temporarily open palisade gate into the arid terrain of western Texas. It was late spring, and the granjeno and prickly pear were brightly visible, with snow peaks beyond. He would be out there soon, riding free and raising hell. If he did this right. It was all up to him. Just like it had been when he swung that axe down onto his father's neck, freeing himself from that other kind of imprisonment. That seemed like about a thousand years ago to Skinner now. But here it was, only 1848, and him with a whole lifetime ahead of him, a lifetime to make his mark on the world the way it had made its mark on him. To get back what it had taken from him, any way that worked.

At midafternoon Skinner received permission to make a trip to the nearby latrine, not far from the mess hall. No guard accompanied mess duty inmates on these excursions, since the area was considered secure. Skinner was alone in there upon arrival, and urinated in a hole in the concrete floor. The pick he had made was secreted under his shirt, in his trousers waistband. When he turned from the urinal, buttoning the gray pewter buttons on his fly, Logan had just walked into the long, malodorous room.

"Skinner," Logan said carefully. He did not think he knew Skinner well enough to call him Mule.

Skinner narrowed little pig eyes on the other man, then let a sour grin move the corner of his mouth. "Logan."

Logan came over to him. "I didn't like pressing you on this. But I got to get out, Skinner. I ain't got no choice in this."

Skinner nodded. "I can understand that. You want to get between your woman's legs a few more times before she kicks off on you. That's it, ain't it?"

Logan's eyes squinted down some. "That ain't it, Skinner. I just got to see her before she goes. I got things to say to her. We been through a lot together. She done for me, she even stole for me. I owe her this."

"Right," Skinner said, having no idea what Logan was talking about.

"I don't like to force myself on no one. But I figured you could probably use some help, anyway. You're going out on the supply wagon, ain't you?"

Skinner nodded. "That's it. I see you heard quite a little."

Logan looked embarrassed.

"Hell, forget it," Skinner said easily. He glanced past Logan, warily. "Come on back here a minute, and let me tell you all about it."

They moved back to the far end of the dank, stinking room, to where there was a long bench over an excrement pit. There was a dividing wall of rough-hewn wood between the bench and the larger part of the room. Skinner took Logan behind this short wall, and Logan leaned up against it. They were not now visible from the entrance to the room.

Skinner faced the smaller man. "Now about that wagon, Logan. I'm going out on it tonight."

Logan grinned uncertainly. "You're going to try hiding in it when it leaves?"

"That's it," Skinner said.

"Won't there be any guards?"

"Not when I make my move. But if anybody gets in the way, I can handle it."

"Yeah?" Logan said.

Skinner pulled the slender pick out from his shirt. "With this," he told the other man.

14

Logan grinned more certainly. "God. But you won't have to actually kill anybody, will you?" Logan was in for extortion, and had never killed a man in his life.

"Would that bother you?" Skinner said, his face somber now.

"Oh, no," Logan said quickly.

"There wouldn't be anything to it," Skinner said, and Logan could hear a new tightness in his voice. "No blood, really." Skinner brought the weapon up to Logan's face, close. "You see, it's not a messy weapon." He turned the point of the pick and casually drove it into Logan's left eyeball.

Logan's eyes saucered, the left one popping and squirting sticky liquid onto his cheek and nose. His hands came up and grabbed at his face and then at Skinner. Skinner pulled the weapon back out of Logan's head, and stepped away from him. Logan began jumping and jerking there on the wood wall, throwing his arms wildly about. Then he slumped heavily to the floor. His legs kicked fitfully at it for a moment, then he was still.

Skinner wiped the weapon clean on Logan's shirt, and returned it to its hiding place at his waist. The body of Logan trembled violently once more, and was still again.

"You see what a clean kill it is?" Skinner said to the corpse.

He bent and lifted the body to the long bench that served as a toilet for the convicts, and propped it there, leaning against the wall behind it, as if Logan were relaxing after a difficult bowel movement.

He then took a piece of paper from a pile on the bench, wiped the sticky stuff off Logan's cheek, and closed Logan's eyelids down. Logan looked as if he had fallen asleep there. As if no violence had occurred.

Skinner threw the soiled paper into the excrement pit, and stood back and inspected his handiwork. "Now ain't that nice and peaceful-like," he said in the sandpaper voice.

Then he turned and casually left the room.

Skinner was wire-tight at supper, though. He had heard a report that the supply wagon had arrived from town, and was even then being unloaded by a special squad of prisoners, who would have their meal later. Wylie, sitting beside him again, ate quickly and would not talk. That was fine with Skinner. He did not want Wylie giving anything away again.

Logan had been discovered in the latrine in late afternoon, and there had been a lot of running about by prison guards, as Skinner had expected, and a body search of prisoners. Skinner had been one of those searched, but he had hidden his weapon in a garbage container, and then retrieved it later. There was word out that the warden would address the entire prison population of several hundred tomorrow morning in the yard, and would pledge to find the killer. But Skinner expected to be gone by then.

It was dark outside when Skinner finished his

meal and returned to his special duty of garbage cleanup before being returned to his cell. He worked with one other man and a guard, but the guard stayed in the mess hall area and did not accompany the detail men out to the carriageway where the garbage was placed until it was picked up and carried outside the compound by the same men twice a week.

Skinner carried two heavy garbage containers out into the carriageway and through it, and the supply wagon was still there. The driver was helping a couple of prisoners with their guard take the last load of tinned goods off the wagon, and then he would be leaving the compound and returning to the nearby town. Skinner's timing was perfect. He returned to the mess hall area, and there was one garbage barrel left. He quickly volunteered to take the last one out.

"You're getting to be a goddamn model prisoner, Skinner," a guard said, grinning at him.

"I don't want no extra time tacked on because I ain't a nice guy," Skinner replied sourly.

Skinner picked up the container, took a sly look around the mess hall area, and headed out to the carriageway.

The prisoners had the wagon unloaded, and were gone, and a bushy-haired driver was just climbing aboard the wagon to drive it out past the guard at the front gate. Skinner put the container down, and looked around. There were no guards visible, and no inmates. The closest persons in sight were the guard at the gate, and the ones in two towers at the

17

corners of the compound. But in this light, they were barely visible as silhouettes. Skinner heard the driver getting set on the seat of the wagon, and picking up the reins of the team of mules that stood out in front of the wagon.

Skinner reached into his clothing, and came up with the wicked-looking pick he had killed Logan with. Then he grabbed at the tailgate of the wagon, and lifted himself aboard at the rear of it. He moved then, hunched over, through the wagon and up to the open front to where the driver sat, under the cover of the canvas top. The driver felt the movement behind him, and turned just as Skinner arrived at his left ear, with the pick poised at the driver's face.

"What the hell!"

Skinner grabbed the fellow's shirt collar with his free hand. "Listen to me, you son of a bitch! One squeak out of you, and you leave here face-down!"

The driver swallowed hard. He was a square-built man with a grizzled beard and cold eyes. "You can't get out of here with a trick like this. Give it up."

Skinner pushed the pick's point against the driver's cheek until it pierced the flesh and drew blood.

"Shit!" the driver spat out.

"Now you listen to me, you stupid bastard, and listen real good," Skinner said in the low, hoarse voice. "You're about one second from having this thing stuck into your brain pan."

The driver finally looked scared.

"Now, you do what I say, you might live through

18

this. You give me away, you get this cold steel. What will it be?"

The driver hesitated, then nodded. "Okay."

"I'm going to throw this tarpaulin over me and hide back here. But I'll be right up behind your seat here. You give any sign to the guard that I'm here, and you die first."

"They look in here," the driver said.

"Let them look," Skinner said. "Now, get this wagon moving. And remember I'll be watching every move you make, every twitch of your goddamn face."

"Right," the driver said solemnly.

Skinner lay down behind him, and drew a tarpaulin over his body. But he could see out the front of it, and had a good view of the driver. "Come on, move!" he hissed out.

The driver jerked the reins over the backs of the mules and they started up. The wagon rumbled very slowly toward the gate of the stockade-type enclosure, and Skinner could see the moon rising behind the palisade wall. It seemed forever that it took to cross the prison yard, and then finally they were at the front gate. The guard came up to the wagon. He was a tough-looking fellow wearing a sheepskin coat and carrying a double-barreled Plains rifle.

"You get it all unloaded?" he said, a question he had asked almost without fail every time the supply wagon left the premises. It was one of those inane remarks that don't require a reply.

"Yep, she's all emptied out," the driver said, and his voice was taut-sounding.

19

The guard eyed him sidewise for a moment, then went to the tailgate and looked into the wagon. He squinted down, saw the tarpaulin Skinner was hiding under, figured it was a pile of cloth and nothing else. He took the gun and poked at some empty boxes near him, to look behind them. Then he came around to the front of the wagon again. Inside under the tarpaulin, Skinner lay with every muscle tight, like a cougar ready to spring.

"Looks like it's going to be a cool, clear night," the guard said.

"Looks that way," the driver agreed. He could almost feel that pick in the back of his head. "I just might stay out awhile tonight. Have a couple of ales in town."

"Put one down for me." The guard grinned. Then he sobered. "Hey, you got a drop of blood on your face there."

The driver's hand went to his face, and he nervously wiped at the pinprick of blood Skinner had put there. Inside the wagon, Skinner prepared to thrust the pick home again.

"Oh, that ain't nothing," the driver said, trying a tight little laugh. "I cut myself shaving earlier, and now the scab just come off. Hell, I'm so damned awkward with anything sharp."

The guard studied his face for a moment, then shrugged. "Well, I guess you better dull that razor down some. Anyway, raise a little hell for me at the saloon when you get there."

The driver relaxed some. "I'll just do that, Quinn," he said with a grin he hoped was convincing. Then he slapped the backs of the mules, and they moved on through the gate.

Inside the wagon, Skinner felt the wheels of the vehicle rumbling on out into the open prairie. He poked his head out through the end of the cloth, and saw the guard closing the big gate behind them.

"God*damn!*" he said softly.

He waited until they were well away from the prison compound, and it had disappeared from sight over a crest of ground, until he crawled out from under his cover. The driver turned to glance at him, and then went back to driving the wagon.

"I did just what you asked," he said.

"And ain't that nice for you," Skinner said, kneeling behind him now, still holding the weapon close to the driver.

"How far you going with me?" the driver asked, as the wagon rumbled along in a well-worn track toward the nearest town.

"Just quit asking questions, and drive," Skinner growled.

The wagon bumped along in the rising moonlight. They passed patches of granjeno and huisache, silvery in the night. It all looked good to Skinner. Anything would look good after spending over a year of his life in that stinking, gray hellhole.

In those moments before he got out of the wagon that evening, Skinner thought of Zachariah McComb, the man who had put him in the Devil's Hole. Skinner and Yuray Lazlo had come upon a cabin in the mountains one day, and had robbery on their minds. They found a man and woman at the cabin, and surprised them. As it turned out later, the woman was Zachariah McComb's squaw, an attractive young Apache that McComb had taken as a wife, but never formally married. The man was a close friend of McComb, who had just come to visit for a couple of days. Like McComb, he was a mountain man, a fellow who made his living by hunting and trapping in and around the South Pass area of the Rockies. McComb was not there when Skinner and Lazlo had arrived, because he was out collecting pelts from his traps.

The friend's name was St. John, and he and McComb went back quite a way together, coming into the area about the same time to make their living away from civilization. The Apache woman was Nalin, the daughter of a Chiricahua Apache, whom McComb had been with for three years.

During McComb's brief absence from that cabin, Skinner and Lazlo killed St. John brutally, stole anything of value at the place, and raped and kidnapped the Indian woman. Skinner and Lazlo later split up, with Lazlo taking Nalin with him when he went to rejoin his cousin's band of renegade Gypsies to the east, out on the flatlands.

McComb tracked Skinner down then, apprehended him in a bitter death struggle, and turned Skinner in to the Texas authorities. Skinner had warned McComb that even though McComb had gotten lucky in subduing him long enough to turn him over to the law, if Skinner actually went behind bars, Skinner would find McComb and kill him. The authorities tried to get Skinner to tell them what had happened to Nalin, but Skinner would not. In fact, he hinted to McComb that she was dead, just to get back at him.

Thinking about all of that now, on this moon-silvery night, Skinner knew what his first project would be, once he was clear of this place. He would seek out McComb, no matter how long it took, and he would kill him. He felt no obligation to confront McComb. He would shoot him in the back, or put him down with a buffalo gun at a long distance, if he had to, to get him. No goddamn half savage like McComb could do what he had to Skinner and live to brag about it.

Skinner looked out ahead of the rumbling wagon, and could just barely see the dim lights of the tiny settlement appearing on the horizon in the blackness. He had seen the place on his way into prison. It was just a few clapboard buildings, and some tentlike structures, and about fifty permanent residents. It stank of pigs and Indians, and Skinner had no intention of stopping there. It would be too dangerous, because that is the first place the warden of Devil's Hole would look. He got to his feet behind the driver, and growled into his ear.

"Okay, hold it up here."

The driver pulled on the reins, and the mules stopped the wagon. Skinner climbed out onto the seat beside the driver.

"This where you're getting off?" the driver said warily.

"No. This is where you're getting off, pig shit."

23

"Me? This is my wagon! I got to take this into town and—"

The driver saw the pick at the last split second. His hand came up to protect himself, but then he felt it slide almost effortlessly into his chest, pierce his breastbone, and then enter his heart.

Skinner released the handle of the pick, and it stuck innocuously out of the driver's shirt. There was no visible blood. The man's eyes looked at Skinner as if he had uttered a particularly insulting epithet against him, and then his jaw was working and his hands were grabbing at the wooden handle of the pick, as if holding it tightly might hold his life in. Then he just collapsed sideways onto the seat, away from Skinner, and part of his torso and his head hung off the wagon seat. The mule on the left of the traces guffered nervously, sensing death in the air.

"Now whose wagon is it, cow dung?" Skinner said in the ugly voice.

There was nobody else out on the trail. Skinner pulled the wagon off into some low-standing mesquite, where it would not be seen easily by any passerby, and then dragged the driver's body into the wagon and covered it with the tarpaulin. That would keep the vultures away for a day or two. He then unharnessed the slimmest of the mules, threw a cloth over its back, and rode it off away from the trail to the southwest.

An hour later, when the cell doors at Devil's Hole were locked for the night, Skinner was finally missed. It took another hour to convince the warden that he was really gone, and a third hour to get ready to go out looking for him. They did not even find the wagon that night. Two days later, with dogs, they finally picked up his trail, but after following it for another day, they gave it up. They knew Skinner was long gone.

They could only hope somebody else returned him to them some day.

Chapter Two

Zachariah McComb did not talk about it much, but he was one-quarter Cherokee. His father's father, back East where the white men and Indians lived in peace and harmony for many years, had impregnated a Cherokee maiden on a business trip, and later had taken the baby son and cared for it. That son became McComb's father, the offspring of an Irish immigrant father and a Native American mother.

McComb's father was named Obadiah, because the grandfather from county Cork had been a Bible reader, and Obadiah had married a second generation Irish girl named Rachel, and together they conceived Zachariah and a sister Megan, with Megan coming along two years after Zachariah. Obadiah enlisted in the militia in 1835, when the trouble between Texas and Mexico erupted, and was at Goliad when Santa Anna came to attack it, after his success at the Alamo. Thinking his family would be safer inside the small fort, Obadiah brought Rachel, Zachariah, and Megan, and they were all there upon Santa Anna's arrival with his troops. Santa Anna promised he would spare all of the defenders if they would just lay down their arms and surrender. The officer in charge at Goliad did so, whereupon Santa Anna immediately issued an order that all at the fort would be summarily executed. Most children were spared, but McComb and little Megan watched in horror, restrained by Mexican soldiers, as Obadiah and Rachel were shot down in cold blood.

That day made a lasting impression on McComb, and changed his entire personality. A few days after the Mexicans left, a neighbor took both children west, with the hope of getting to Santa Fe. Everybody died on that trip except McComb. Megan was buried out on the prairie in an unmarked grave, dead of the same fever that killed the others. McComb recovered, was taken in by Apaches, and lived with them for three years. With them he learned to ride, hunt, and trap like any Indian, and when he left them, he was generally regarded as the most skilled of the young braves of the village. It was then that McComb went into the mountains on his own, to be away from men and civilization that he no longer trusted, and earn his living in the Indian way.

In the ensuing years, McComb became the very best in his line of work, and his name was mentioned with those of William Sublette, Joe Walker, and Jim Bridger. As he had done with the Apaches, he would go out from his home base for weeks and months at a time, hunting sheep and buffalo and trapping beaver and ermine. The Apaches called these forays Long Hunts, and they and later the Shoshoni gave him the Indian name of Long Hunter. McComb's best friends were Indians, and the trapper St. John, whom Skinner had viciously murdered, later. When McComb had arrived at a point in his life when he hungered for a woman's comfort, he chose one from his old Apache village, and she was a pretty girl. Nalin was fine-featured and gracefully built, like a doe. She had tended to McComb's wants and desires for almost three years off and on, returning to her village for long periods. There had been no children from this close relationship, and no promises of permanence on the part of McComb. He did not want to be tied to any other person, male or female, and preferred to be alone for long periods of time. Now, in this spring of 1848, with McComb still not thirty years old, he was alone again, but not by choice, and he presumed Nalin dead.

It was several weeks after Skinner's escape from prison now, and mid-April, and McComb had gotten all his furs and pelts together at his cabin not far from South Pass, and taken them all down to Bear Lake, near Fort Bridger, where that year's local trade fair was being held. These gatherings of trappers, buyers, and Indians from the area used to be the biggest event of the year, in the 1830s, and had been called rendezvous, and they had lasted a month and involved thousands of traders. Now the gatherings were pale imitations of those larger fairs, and there were far fewer of them, since the big

28

demand for beaver pelts, and to a lesser extent for ermine, had diminished. But the trading was still better than at Fort Bridger or Fort Bonneville.

McComb arrived on the second day of the gathering, putting up a tent on the lake. There were about fifty trappers, holed up in tents, lean-tos, and wagons, or sleeping in the open, their numbers matched by those of Indians who came for the same purpose—Shoshoni, Crow, Flatheads, Nez Percé, and others. Then there were the buyers and traders from the towns, who came every year just for this fair. Some of them looked out of place, with their eastern clothing and watches on glittery gold chains. They would set up in fancy wagons and large tents, and stay most of a week to buy and trade for such goods as buffalo robes, ermine skins, bear claw necklaces, and frozen elk meat. There was always a lot of drinking, card playing, bargaining in loud voices, and fighting. Every year two or three traders were carried off to the nearest fort in a pine box. The Indians whooped and hollered and had parades and dancing. They also held sober councils among themselves, and white men were not welcome. What the mountain men and Indians got back for their valuable furs and pelts were cigars, liquor, ammunition, clothing, utensils for daily living, mules, horses, food, and sometimes silver or gold.

On the day that McComb set up his tent on the bank of the lake and spread his furs out on the ground for traders to view, the trade fair was in full swing. Shoshonis strutted about in full dress regalia, eagle feathers and all, and big men in buckskin clothes walked past carrying long guns, with strings of beaver pelts slung over their shoulders. There were also some Conestogas camped at the fair, settlers on their way to Oregon or California, and wanting to replenish their supplies, and there were a couple of Gypsy caravans, with their gaudily painted wood sides. Gypsies had been seen for years at these sites, where they traded mostly with Indians. Some of them were recent immigrants from Europe, and spoke local Indian languages as well as or better than English. Many Indians would not deal with them, though, because some renegade Gypsy bands had the reputation of being thieves, and of kidnapping Indian children to sell later as slaves to other tribes. McComb, because of his time with the Apaches, was distrustful of all Gypsies, and that distrust had been intensified when he learned that the man who had been with Emmett Skinner was a Gypsy named Lazlo, and who to this time had escaped McComb's retribution.

It took McComb most of a long, sunny morning to set up his tent among the other traders and get his goods ready to display. It was generally known that McComb's furs and skins were of top quality, and had been prepared well for sale, so traders began swarming to his location by late morning, before he was really ready for them, and began trading for his goods. He traded away some of the best ermine pelts he had ever had, and received in return a sturdy young mule with good teeth, a pair of store-made boots, a case of Red Top rye whiskey, and some gold tokens minted by a California mining company.

Since McComb had holed up in his mountain cabin near the great South Pass, he had become well known by the Shoshonis and Crow and quite close to one area Shoshoni tribe whose leader was a chief named Silver Wolf. Silver Wolf and his warrior son Iron Knife had hunted with McComb, and slept in his cabin, and he had shared celebration feasts with them in their village, which was located on a creek west of the Great Salt Lake a hundred miles.

It was about noontime on that day of McComb's arrival at the Bear Lake trade fair that Iron Knife surprised McComb by appearing at his campsite on the water's edge. Usually, Silver Wolf's people steered clear of these trade fairs, because of all the drinking and guns in evidence. But Iron Knife had persuaded his rather elderly father that he could stay out of trouble.

McComb saw him approaching, looking straight and regal, and a grin crossed McComb's face. He had been sitting on a camp stool, surrounded by his skins on the ground, sucking on a stogie cigar, when Iron Knife came up, with two women close on his heels, carrying strings of furs.

"Well, I'll be damned," McComb said easily. He rose from the stool and came to greet Iron Knife, discarding the cigar.

McComb was an athletically built, rather slim but muscular young man who was only twenty-eight but looked older. He was over six feet tall, which made him look down on most other men, and he had dark brown hair and a full beard of the same color. His hair was long, almost to shoulder length, and his eyes were a deep sky blue. The few women who had seen him up close had considered him ruggedly handsome, but McComb was completely unaware of that. He had never womanized, and the Apache woman Nalin had been only the third woman he had ever lain with.

He wore buckskin shirt and pants, with high, stovepipe boots on his feet, and a dark Stetson, crumpled and trail-worn, on his head, with an eagle feather stuck in its band. His antelope buckskin shirt was caught at the waist by a thick cartridge belt, on which McComb carried a Patterson-Colt revolver that he kept well oiled but rarely used. In his life he had had to kill seven times, with three of the deaths Indians who had gone renegade. He looked upon killing rather unemotionally, like an Apache, and part of that feeling about it stemmed from the fact that he had witnessed both of his parents' deaths, when they had been shot down before him in that bloody drama at Goliad.

Iron Knife approached him rather soberly and they met at the edge of McComb's ground display. "I greet you in friendship, Long Hunter," the Indian said in Shoshoni, which McComb understood.

They raised their hands in the traditional greeting.

"May our friendship outlast the arrival of a thousand new moons," McComb replied in the Indian's language.

It was all very formal for a moment, in the Indian way. Then both men broke into smiles, and embraced each other vigorously. Iron Knife was shorter than McComb, but also very muscular, and broader through the chest. He wore rawhide clothing not far different from McComb's, and a headband with two large eagle feathers set in it. He had a rather long, aquiline face, and piercing brown eyes. His two women, rather short and round-faced, stood quietly behind him and grinned but did not speak.

McComb lapsed into English, since both Iron Knife and his father were fluent in it. "Damn good to see you again, Iron Knife. It must be six months since you stopped past my cabin."

Iron Knife nodded. "And you have been very busy, I see, trapping our Shoshoni ermine and beaver."

The reference to Shoshoni ownership of area game was a standing joke between Iron Knife and McComb, and McComb grinned widely at the mention of it. The Indians had never thought in terms of anything in nature belonging to them, until the white man had invaded their tribal territories. Then some of them, primarily Crow and never Silver Wolf's people, had begun claiming the land and the game in it, and even its rivers and streams, as their own.

"I looked carefully for Shoshoni brands on my ermine," McComb replied seriously, going along with the joke.

"Then peace will reign between us," Iron Knife

concluded. "How is it with you, my good friend? Have you been well?"

"Well enough," McComb replied, knowing the Indian was referring to McComb's loss of Nalin. "And how is your father?"

"He surprises everyone with his strength," Iron Knife told him. "He asked me to convey his good wishes to you."

"Please return the favor," McComb said.

Iron Knife moved around the perimeter of the spread-out furs and skins. "You are a great hunter, McComb," he said. He used McComb's right name interchangeably with the Indian one. "You have beaten me again on the ermine." He bent and studied a dark brown buffalo robe, perfect in quality. "I know this animal. I tracked it for weeks. You make me envious."

McComb smiled. "Do you still keep a supply of iron knives for trading?"

The Indian nodded. "Of course. I began it as a child, and now it is expected of me."

"If you think it's fair, you may have the robe for five of your iron-bladed, hardwood-handled knives."

Iron Knife caught McComb's eye. "It is not fair, Long Hunter. The robe is worth much more than that."

McComb shook his head sidewise. "Don't tell me the value of my own goods, my friend." He picked the heavy robe up, folded it, and handed it to Iron Knife. "Here. For all the good brotherhood between us."

Iron Knife hesitated, then took the robe. He caressed the fur gently, then turned and gave the robe to his nearest woman. He spoke to her in Shoshoni, and she gave him a rawhide bag with knives in it. He turned and gave that to McComb.

"Thank you for the trade," McComb said.

"Our friendship grows with each meeting." Iron Knife smiled. He put a tanned hand on McComb's shoulder. "I have news for you, my brother." His long face had gone serious.

McComb looked at him quizzically. "What news?"

"When your friend was killed, the man who escaped your law was named Lazlo, yes?"

"That's right," McComb said.

"He has been seen by our kinsmen," Iron Knife went on.

McComb's bearded face went very somber. "Where?"

"To the east, beyond South Pass. There was some trading with the Gypsies, and one of them was called by his people Lazlo."

"Do you know where these Gypsies were heading?" McComb asked. He had already casually checked out the two wagons at the trade fair site, and none of the Gypsies there admitted ever having heard of Yuray Lazlo.

Iron Knife shook his head. "My kinsmen did not know."

McComb sighed. "Well. I'll keep my ears open, Iron Knife. And thanks for the help."

"We are brothers," Iron Knife said. "Well, I must

35

try to trade my furs, Long Hunter. But before I go later today, maybe we might smoke a pipe together."

"I'll look for some makings," McComb told him.

Before Iron Knife left, he and McComb had another long visit, squatting on the ground with a buffalo robe under them. McComb was accustomed to primitive living. Because he mixed hunting with trapping, he was out on the hardship trail for long periods, away from his cabin in the mountains, eating soda biscuits from a flour sack and boiling coffee in a tomato tin. He liked that life much better than the kind he found when he visited towns and settlements, and had to put up with so-called civilized folks.

At dusk, just after Iron Knife left, McComb met several other trappers that he had come to know over the recent years. A group of Nez Percé Indians were having a celebration not far down the lakeshore, and there was dancing and singing and a lot of noise. It was all very gala in the evenings at the trade fairs, when the business day was over. McComb was just laying out a bedroll inside the small tent, in preparation for sleep, when his last visitor arrived. It was another mountain man named Will Beaumont, a trapper who operated not far from McComb. He was a thin, closemouthed fellow who usually did not say more than a half-dozen words in any encounter with him. This evening, though, he was a bit more talkative.

"McComb," he said when he arrived at Mc-

Comb's tent. He carried a Plains rifle under his arm, and wore a coonskin cap.

"Beaumont," McComb replied, turning to him. A couple hundred yards away, there was drumming and singing coming from the Nez Percé encampment. "How you been?"

Beaumont nodded. "Saw your skins. Good quality."

"Thanks," McComb said. "Doing any business?" McComb's furs were almost gone already.

"Some," Beaumont said. He was an older fellow, with gray in his hair and beard, and he had been at his trade for a lot of years, but he would never be the hunter or trapper that McComb was, and he knew it.

"That's good," McComb said.

"I seen Davis over at the Shoshoni spread. There must be cadavers up at Fort Bonneville with quarters on their eyes that look better."

"I spoke to him," McComb said. "He looks bad, all right. I guess he's got the mountain lung." He watched Beaumont's face. Usually the other man was not so sociable.

"That feller Skinner, that you put behind bars."

McComb looked at him.

"He's out."

McComb frowned heavily. "Are you sure?"

"I got it from a drifter that had been to Devil's Hole. He escaped. Killed two men."

McComb mused about that for a moment. "Son of a bitch," he finally said.

"Another thing," Beaumont said. He stuck a wad

37

of tobacco into his mouth, and began chewing on it. "I come through South Pass a few days ago. On the far side I run onto a Gypsy campsite. No doubt what it was, it had a stink to it."

McComb looked up at him.

"It wasn't one of these wagons, these couldn't got here so fast."

McComb's patience wore thin. "What about it?" He recalled that Lazlo had been identified with a Gypsy caravan on the far side of South Pass.

"I took a good look at that camp area," Beaumont told him.

McComb gave him a look. "Get on with it, Beaumont."

Beaumont appraised McComb's face. McComb was considered a kind of half savage, even by other mountain men. McComb had once beaten a trader to death with his bare hands, because the man had insulted Nalin. It had taken four men to drag McComb off the trader, but by then it was too late. It had been John Fremont who had started McComb's reputation by announcing to anyone who would listen that McComb could ride like a Comanche, track like an Apache, and drink like an old country Irishman. What Lieutenant Fremont had not said, but which everybody in the South Pass-Bear Lake area knew, was that McComb was a man you did not cross. It was only because another trapper prevented him that he had not killed Emmett Skinner when he caught up with him, instead of turning him in to the law.

"Don't get all stiff-necked," Beaumont said warily. "What I'm trying to tell you is, I found some interesting stuff at that camp."

"Like what?" McComb said in a subdued voice, through the thick beard. He was trying to control his temper.

"Like a couple of Apache things."

McComb frowned.

"Your woman was Apache, waren't she?"

"That's right," McComb said carefully.

Beaumont reached into a pouch hanging from his buckskins, and opened it slowly. McComb watched him. Finally Beaumont drew out two items from the pouch, and McComb's face changed. "Let me see that stuff," he growled. He reached and took the items from Beaumont without asking.

Beaumont looked hurt, but said nothing. McComb was looking at a turquoise Apache pendant that had come off a necklace, and a primitive bone comb.

"My God," he said.

"They're hers, ain't they?" Beaumont grinned.

McComb did not hear him. "She might be alive," he said somberly.

"That's what I figured," Beaumont said.

McComb looked up at him. "Exactly where did you find these?"

"The campsite was on that small side trail that leads into the pass from the east. I'd say a couple hours' ride from where it joins up with the main trail."

"How do you know for sure it was a Gypsy camp?"

39

"I'm telling you. The stink from that stuff they cook was still in the air. And the wheels on them wagons is different, like these here at the lake. I can spot them anywhere. It was Gypsies, all right. No doubt in my mind."

"I heard that Lazlo used to run with a renegade band," McComb said to himself. "That son of a bitch run back to them and took Nalin with him."

Beaumont studied McComb's face as emotions of various kinds drifted through and across it. "You owe me, McComb."

McComb looked over at him. Oh, shit, he thought.

"You do owe me," Beaumont said quietly.

What a bastard, McComb thought. He glanced toward the pile of furs behind him, that he intended to take into the tent for the night. "Take your pick of the buffalo robes and ermine pelts," he said quietly.

"You mean it?" Beaumont said with a grin.

"Do it," McComb said gruffly. His tanned face under the beard, weathered and lined from exposure to sun and wind, made him look closer to forty than thirty.

"Much obliged," Beaumont said, knowing how good McComb's skins were. He pawed through the stuff for a couple of minutes, took a robe and an ermine pelt, and headed off toward his own sleeping roll. As he headed out, McComb called after him.

"Beaumont."

The other man turned back.

"Thanks."

Beaumont nodded, and disappeared into the tents of the encampment.

Staring after him, McComb realized that something that had always had a tight grip on his chest inside him had released its hold just a little since Beaumont's visit to him, and he could look up at the starry sky and breathe just a little more easily than he had in quite some time. Maybe Skinner and Lazlo had not killed Nalin. Maybe they had just kidnapped her, and Lazlo had sold her to his Gypsy friends, or kept her for his own woman. That was nothing to rejoice about, but if she was alive, McComb would be grateful.

He could not stay at the fair. He would leave first thing tomorrow morning, to return to his cabin and leave his goods there before setting off into the high mountains to see if he could locate the Gypsy caravan that had left these Apache relics behind.

He had no time to lose.

Every moment could be important to Nalin.

That night passed slowly for McComb. He kept dreaming and waking up, and the dreaming was all about that bleak day at South Pass when he had returned to his cabin to find his friend murdered and his woman gone. It was a day he would never forget. Like the one at Goliad.

The following morning, before most of the encampment was awake and up, McComb packed up his goods and gear onto his two mules, mounted his pinto stallion, and rode off into the gray mist of the Green River Valley.

It was a two-day ride back to his cabin, and there was still some snow to ride through. He knew he had lost some business by leaving early, but finding that Gypsy wagon train was now the most important thing in McComb's world. If Nalin was still alive, every day she was with those particular Gypsies could be another ordeal of terror for her. Even though Gypsies dealt a lot with Indians, even the better ones had little respect for the red man. Consequently, Nalin would be like a chattel to them, and be treated as livestock, or worse.

McComb rode through mountain country for those two days, with snow peaks all around him. It was his kind of country, with its craggy cliffs and sweet-smelling pines and mountain lions. He could barely remember any life before this. In fact, he had a traumatic amnesia related to his young life before the awful tragedy at Goliad. His life with the Apaches and Shoshonis, and his isolated existence in these high peaks, were his entire personal history, in his own mind. To the few people who ever got to know him, those factors had combined to create a quiet, rather introspective loner, who could appear more like a savage at times than a civilized man, but whose moral values toward those who knew him well were bedrock solid.

Throughout the few saloons and gambling halls that had sprung up in settlement forts and tiny villages in the area, McComb had gained an awesome reputation as a knife fighter, and was said to know

"Indian tricks" still unknown to the white man. McComb had had to kill a buffalo hunter turned drifter one snowy night at Fort Davy Crockett, because the man had threatened him with an old muzzle-loading, smoothbore pistol, and everyone present had been impressed that McComb had taken a lead ball to the ribs, disarmed the other man, and then killed him with only a Jim Bowie knife. There had been a couple other, nonfatal encounters similar to that one at other places, and now most men kept clear of the rather tall, wiry man who often entered a store or saloon in a bearskin coat and a winter coon cap, looking almost primordial in his thick beard and wild hair, usually carrying his Collier double-barreled shotgun under his arm.

McComb arrived at his cabin in midmorning of the third day from Bear Lake. The cabin was nestled in a secluded spot at a height of ten thousand feet, and you could not find it unless you knew exactly where it was. On that brisk spring morning, McComb rounded an outcropping of rock and reined in on the pinto stallion he rode. The mules trailing behind caught up in shallow snow and also stopped.

The stallion guffered, and light fog rose from its nostrils. McComb was staring toward the cabin, his only home since his days with the Apaches.

The cabin was built so that half of it was belowground level, with the sod roof rising above that level only about five feet. There was a thick door at the front, on leather hinges, but no windows. The ground it sat in rose uphill slightly to the rear of it, so that only about two feet of its rear wall showed above ground. It was made of hand-hewn hardwood logs, and sealed with a clay mud. There were times, in the winter, when McComb was obliged to dig out, or dig to get in when he returned from setting traps.

At this moment, McComb sat his mount with a scowl on his face. Smoke lofted from the cabin's chimney, and curled into a clear springtime sky. There were a few trappers who had permission to use the cabin, but none of them were in the area now, they were all at the trade fair.

"What the hell," McComb said quietly.

He dismounted from the pinto, and picketed it to a low, scraggly cedar tree. The mules were already tethered to the stallion. On either flank of the stallion were saddle scabbards on its irons, and they held the Collier shotgun and McComb's buffalo gun. McComb moved around the stallion to its right flank, and unsheathed the shotgun. Reaching into a saddle pouch, he retrieved two cartridges and loaded both barrels of the gun. Then he headed on up the gradual slope to the cabin, only thirty yards away.

As he approached it, he heard a small noise inside, and then he noticed the ragged-looking, small mare mustang picketed at the far side of the place.

The door stood wide open. McComb looked around, and saw no evidence that there was anybody outside the cabin. He moved slowly to the door, off to one side. There was the sound of a pan clinking against a utensil, from inside.

McComb stepped quickly inside, the shotgun out in front of him.

The one-room cabin was flooded with sunlight from outside. Across at a far wall, a man whirled quickly, drawing a sidearm at his hip. He looked in shock down the barrels of the shotgun, froze for a moment with the pistol pointed at the floor, and then dropped the weapon.

He was a dirty, ugly man, wearing a mixture of clothing styles that fit him awkwardly, and a stubble of beard on his lined face. His small eyes revealed abject fear, as he focused on the wild-looking figure in the doorway.

Now that he saw his adversary was disarmed, McComb's blue eyes let his gaze travel about the room. It was almost unrecognizable. Cooking ware had been thrown everywhere, blankets were on the floor, bottles had been opened and their contents strewn over the hardwood planks underfoot. Other bottles had been smashed against walls. The double-decker bunk on the wall to the left had been turned over onto its side, as had a table and chairs. There was also a stink of feces in the place.

A low growl began in McComb's throat. In the Apache village where he had been raised, a violation of this kind in a warrior's tipi or wickiup was punished by death, and McComb lived pretty closely by Apache standards of conduct.

Almost before the intruder realized what was happening, McComb had sprung across the small room and swung the big gun at the other man. The fellow uttered an outcry, and threw a hand up in defense, but the long barrel of the shotgun cracked against the side of his head, and across his shoulder, and he cried out a muffled yell and went down. McComb threw the shotgun down.

McComb stood over him, and his face had changed completely. A cold, very hard look had come into the blue eyes, and his usually rather handsome face had gone straight-lined under the beard. This was the face they had seen in that saloon that winter night when McComb had killed violently with the knife. The knife was in a sheath on his cartridge belt at this moment, and his Patterson-Colt rested on his right hip. But he did not go for either weapon. He reached and pulled the other man up by his coat front with one sinewy, muscular arm. The intruder stared into those iceberg-cold eyes, and bled at the side of his head, and tried to catch his breath, and knew he had never seen eyes quite like these.

"Wait!" he gasped out. "I—"

McComb threw a heavy fist into his face, holding him up. Then he hit him again, and again. The intruder's face was a bloody pulp suddenly, crimson inching from his nose, his mouth, his left eye. McComb grabbed him with both hands, and heaved him bodily against the nearest wall. The other man hit there hard, and bone cracked audibly in his right arm. He yelled out again, slumping to the floor in a crumpled heap. McComb came over him and kicked him savagely in the side, fracturing ribs.

McComb intended to beat him to death.

The intruder spat out two front teeth, with some blood. *"Wait!"* he gritted out. *"I — didn't do it!"*

McComb stood over him menacingly. There was something behind his eyes now that had crawled up from some deep place inside him, where it usually rested quiet like a caged animal. He was breathing a bit irregularly, and he was geared emotionally to break and mash and maul. He paused, though, now.

"What did you say?" The words had such force behind them that the other man feared to respond. But he must, to have a chance of saving his life.

"I didn't — wreck the — cabin."

The thing in McComb's eyes changed subtly, and he stood there letting that sink in for a moment.

"No?" he finally said, unbelieving.

"I swear — on my mother's — grave." He coughed and more blood came up. He moved slightly, and cried out softly in raw pain from his broken arm. Every time he breathed, his ribs sent more knives of pain into his chest.

"I been here — just an hour. It was like this — when I come in."

McComb felt the thing sliding back down inside him, to the place where it hid from the world. "You was eating my food," he grated out. He jerked a thumb toward the counter on the wall where the pan sat, with tinned carrots in it.

The fellow nodded. "I ain't eat in a couple days. I was — heading toward South Pass and got lost."

McComb stared into the man's eyes, in the way Indians do. Finally, he believed him.

"There's a paper over there on the counter. I can't read. But maybe it was left — by them that done this."

McComb glanced toward a handwritten note that lay rumpled on the counter. He hesitated, then reached down and pulled the intruder to his feet. Another yell came from the man.

"You're lucky I didn't finish you off when I walked in," McComb said to him then, in a controlled voice. His eyes looked different now, more human.

"I just took — some grub," the fellow said very quietly.

"Get on your goddamn mount, and get out of here," McComb said to him, releasing him from an iron grip.

"You busted me up. I need tending to," the drifter complained. But then he saw the look in McComb's eyes. "Okay. I'll go."

The man stumbled out of the cabin, and McComb watched him awkwardly mount the mustang and then ride off sullenly into the snowy rocks. When he was finally gone, McComb went back inside the cabin, and looked around again. It was a complete mess. It would take hours to clean it up, and even then he had lost valuable supplies that would be hard to replace. He went over to an end wall, to a small fireplace where the intruder had built a fire, and kicked the coals up with a hand-wrought poker. "Son of a bitch," he muttered.

48

He walked over to the counter, and picked up the crumpled piece of paper there, and his eyes narrowed down as he read.

YOUR A LUKY MAN MCCOMB. IF YOU WAS HEAR, YOUD BE SPATERED ALL OVERE THIS PLACE, JIST LIK YOUR GOODS. BUT IM GOING TO FINDE YOU MISTER. I TOLDE YOU. DONT EXPECT NO FAIRE FITE. YOU PROBLY WONT NO WHEN IT HAPENS. YOU THINK ABUT THAT AT NITE, MCCOMB. YOU JIST THINK ABUT IT.

EMMETT SKINNER

McComb looked up from the paper, and stared past it at the wall. Will Beaumont's information had been right. Skinner was out.

McComb crushed the paper in his right fist, and then threw it violently into the fireplace. He walked over to the doorway, leaned against the jamb, and gazed out across the patches of snow.

This promised to be an interesting spring.

Chapter Three

It took McComb the rest of that day to put the cabin in order, and all during those hours of cleaning up, he remembered over and over that muggy, overcast day when he had finally caught up with Emmett "Mule" Skinner.

He had been disappointed that Skinner was alone, because he had known there were two men at his cabin on that day of death, and had learned later who they were, when Lazlo and Skinner had gotten whiskied up and bragged about the escapade at McComb's cabin. They also admitted sexual attacks on Nalin, but there was no evidence they had taken her with them. By the time McComb found Skinner, he was alone, and McComb presumed that Nalin was dead. Skinner had reinforced that notion, later, by suggesting that she would not last long alive with Lazlo.

On that day of the confrontation with Skinner, another trapper had joined McComb temporarily in the hunt, out on the trail, and they had lost Skinner's spoor. They had split up to pick up the trail again, and when McComb had found Skinner, he had been alone. Skinner had realized immediately who he was, and had fired a sidearm at McComb and hit him. That did not stop McComb. He came on through the gunfire like a charging cougar, and knocked Skinner on his back, and Skinner lost his weapon.

It was a hand-to-hand combat then, and Skinner outweighed McComb by quite a lot, but it did not take long to learn that he might find no comfort in that small advantage. Skinner, who always fought with wild abandon himself, was overwhelmed by the fury of the man he suddenly found himself rolling on the ground with, on that warm day. He found McComb's face with his big, thick fists, and made it bloody, but McComb didn't act as if he even knew he was hurt. Finally, McComb's furious assault wore Skinner down, and at that point McComb was bent on killing Skinner. But the other trapper arrived just as Skinner, battered and bloody, had given up on surviving the fight, and pulled McComb off him, saying Skinner should be judged by the law. McComb almost turned on his own trapper friend then, so great was his resolve to kill, but finally he allowed the other man prevail, and they took Skinner to the Texas law.

Skinner had never been so outfought and humbled as he was in that fight, and he had not suffered long enough under McComb's Apachelike wrath to have his fear of McComb overshadow his great anger and frustration at being beaten badly and then turned in to the law to go behind bars. Skinner was smart enough, though, to know that in his vengeance he would not risk his own skin against this half-savage trapper. Skinner intended to kill him in a way that gave McComb no chance to defend himself, and he intended that McComb's death, if possible, be slow and painful. This had become a kind of obsession with him, in those dark days behind bars at Devil's Hole, and nothing else mattered to him quite as much as his plan to kill McComb.

McComb knew nothing of that obsession, of course, as he prepared to leave his cabin once again, and head out for the South Pass to find the Gypsies that Iron Knife and Beaumont had told him about. He knew only that Skinner had sworn revenge to him openly, as McComb turned him over to the Texas authorities, and that now Skinner was threatening him with written messages that possibly should or should not be taken seriously.

At any rate, McComb's focus now must be on an attempt to learn if Nalin was still alive, and if she was, to rescue her from Lazlo and his band of renegade Gypsies.

With that in mind, he left the cabin the very next morning, took his mules to another trapper closer to South Pass and paid him to keep them for him while he was gone, and rode off on the black-and-white stallion toward the high snow of South Pass. The Sharps buffalo rifle and the Collier shotgun rode snugly in their saddle scabbards, and he carried the breech-loading revolver and the Bowie knife on his gun belt.

He was ready for trouble.

* * *

Fort Bridger, sitting on a branch of the Green River not far from Bear Lake and the trade fair that had just ended, was a fortified settlement that had by now outgrown its palisade protection and had spread out over hundreds of acres on the lush riverbank. The center of the settlement was still enclosed by the old wall, and all public buildings except for a couple of gaming halls stood inside the enclosure. There was a kind of town hall, a store, and a saloon. Banking was still done by individuals. Fort owners lived inside the enclosure, also. Outside, there were cabins, lean-tos, and tents. The gaming houses outside were in cabin-tent structures.

There was some mining done in the area, and there were prospectors who had found gold in the local rivers. But it was the fur trade that supported the fort, and most of the outsiders whom the fort saw were trappers and hunters. The fort also did a brisk business, though, in outfitting and supplying wagon trains on their way West, and East.

Emmett Skinner had been at Fort Bridger for only a few hours as other men began avoiding him when he appeared anywhere. The local saloon had several rooms to rent upstairs, and that was where Skinner stayed upon his arrival. By that time, he had already killed a rider on the trail, and stolen his entire belongings, including a dun mare with all its saddlery and irons, and a Derringer Navy 1843 .54 caliber pistol, with a revolving cylinder. He wore the gun on his right hip, talked loudly, and swaggered about as if he owned the place.

He was frustrated that he had not been able to sneak up on McComb at his cabin and back-shoot him. He had come on down here from South Pass in the hope of finding McComb, or at least finding someone who might lead Skinner to him.

There was no law yet at Fort Bridger. In fact, there was none for hundreds of miles around. Consequently, locals had to be able to defend themselves against bad men who drifted in, and if they did not feel able, they kept quiet, steered clear, and hoped that those individuals did not stay long.

That is the way the locals felt about Skinner. He had begun asking about McComb as soon as he arrived, and found out immediately that McComb was not there. But he still hoped he would run onto someone who knew McComb's whereabouts. Up until the evening of his second night there, nobody had been willing to talk to Skinner. But then, while Skinner was in the saloon about midevening, a trapper drifted in, a man who had just arrived at the fort. He came and leaned against a rough-hewn bar not far from where Skinner stood, and ordered a whiskey from a small, potbellied barkeep. Skinner turned and stared at him as he received the drink.

"You a mountain man, are you?" Skinner asked in the gritty voice.

The other man looked over at him. He was of average height, and rather bony and thin. His face was lean and long, and he wore a light-colored mustache almost the same color as his weathered face. His name was Owens, and like McComb, he preferred not to talk with others when he came into a center of so-called civilization.

"What if I am?" he finally said.

Skinner's eyes clouded over some. "I reckon a man wouldn't sneak around in them high rocks skinning beaver if he was fit for anything else," he said evenly.

The trapper glanced over at him again. Skinner was a lot bigger than him, and he did not want any trouble. "You could look at it that way," he said. He swigged part of the whiskey.

"I don't see no other way," Skinner said, a hard grin on his beefy face. He swigged a drink down in one gulp, and wiped a hand across his mouth. "Set me up again, barkeep."

The bartender gave Skinner a mildly reproachful look, and poured him another drink. Skinner studied it for a moment. The trapper named Owens hunched over his drink and hoped Skinner would go away.

"I wouldn't mind so much if all of you boys didn't stink so much of guts and dried blood," Skinner finally added.

The bartender began to look nervous. "Let's not get all juicy now, boys. Take it outside if you got any quarrels."

Skinner looked at him. "Shut up," he said.

There were two miners sitting over at a table near the door. They exchanged looks, rose from the table, and left through the slatted swinging doors.

Owens looked at Skinner for the third time. "Why don't you let it go?" he said quietly. "I just want to drink my liquor in peace and quiet."

Skinner's face darkened in menace. "You telling me I'm too loud?" he grated out. "Or maybe just too crude for your genteel taste?"

Owens was not armed. He glanced at the Derringer revolver on Skinner's hip, and his gut tightened inside him. "I didn't say that," he said almost inaudibly. "Just let it go."

The bartender had backed away from the bar, and was standing against the shelves of bottles behind the bar, not daring to speak now. His gaze darted from Skinner to Owens and back to Skinner. He and those two were the only ones in the place now, and he suddenly wished there were more customers about.

Skinner adjusted himself more comfortably against the bar, facing Owens squarely now. "I guess you'd know just about all them other beaver skinners that operate around this neck of the woods."

Owens met his gaze with reluctance. "Some of them, if you mean trappers."

Skinner grunted. "You know a fellow by the name of McComb?"

Owens's eyes squinted down slightly. He knew McComb fairly well, and had seen him at Bear Lake at the trade fair. But he could not imagine that he had met the acquaintance of a man like this one. "I just might," Owens said cagily.

Skinner frowned. "Don't straddle no fence, beaver man, or you're going to get into my craw. You seen him hereabouts lately?"

Owens hesitated, appreciating the threat behind Skinner's words. He did not want big trouble, to protect another trapper he saw only once or twice a year. "He was at the Bear Lake fair. I ain't seen him since then."

Skinner thought about that for a moment. McComb must have been at the trade fair when Skinner was at his cabin. Skinner had wrongfully thought that McComb might be out on one of those long hunts that could take weeks or months. Skinner realized now that McComb might have returned to the cabin after he was there, and he might still be there.

"What do you want him for?" the trapper said suspiciously.

Skinner met his look with a hard one. "I want to cut his liver out and have it for supper some dark night," he said gutturally.

Owens swallowed sudden fear back into his throat, and glanced at the bartender. He was no fighter, and he felt a real menace in Skinner's manner. "Well. That's all I know, mister." He threw a couple of coins onto the bar. "That's for the drink, barkeep."

Skinner pulled the Derringer Navy revolver free of its holster and aimed it at the trapper's chest. "You ain't leaving just yet, are you?"

Owens stared at the gun, then met Skinner's brittle gaze. "I thought I might."

"You think maybe McComb might go back to

that cabin after the Bear Lake thing?" he said ominously.

"He might," Owens said. "I wouldn't know."

"You mean you don't want to tell me, ain't that it?"

"I ain't armed, mister. I don't want any trouble."

"I just got the suspicion you might light out of here and ride up to McComb's place to tell him I'm coming," Skinner said slowly. "You wouldn't do that now, would you."

Actually, Owens had decided he might ride past McComb's place, to tell him about this crazy-acting drifter. But he was not going to tell Skinner that. "That ain't none of my business," he said nervously.

"That don't really answer my question now, does it?" Skinner persisted with a harsh grin.

Owens averted his gaze. "I ain't got no plans to ride up there. You can rest easy on that score." He started past Skinner, but Skinner barred his way. The bartender found he was holding his breath, back against the shelves.

Owens found some anger in him now, and his face crimsoned slightly. "I don't like to be boned by nobody, gun or not," he said with false bravado. "I ain't trying to throw mud on you, mister, but it ain't hardly right to ask after a man like you're doing. I don't want to be no part of it."

Skinner surprisingly grinned. "Hell, I won't bother you no more with it, then." He let the sidearm drop to his side.

Owens relaxed some inside, and nodded to Skinner, then moved around him and headed for the doorway. He got halfway there, when he heard Skinner's voice call after him.

"Oh, yeah. One more thing, mountain man."

When the trapper turned, his eyes widened as he saw Skinner's revolver aimed at him once again. While he was still reacting inside to that hard fact, Skinner squeezed the trigger of the Derringer and there was an explosion in the room that shook hand-rived timbers in the ceiling and made the bartender's ears ring. Owens was hit in center chest, picked up off his feet, and dumped in an awkward heap near the swinging doors. His right hand went to the hole in his chest, and his body shuddered all over, and he was lifeless there.

"Mary Mother of God!" the bartender whispered.

Skinner did not hear him. He went and stood over the dead man for a moment, then reholstered the gun. He was breathing shallowly, and little thrills of pleasure were coursing through his insides, not unlike when he was with a woman.

"Now we both know where you'll be tonight," he murmured.

A moment later, he had left the place, and shortly thereafter he had left the fort. He would make another trip to McComb's cabin, and if he was not there, he would pick up his trail and find him.

Then the buzzards would feed on McComb's corpse.

* * *

The next several days in South Pass were sunny and cool. McComb passed through the snow-streaked area with its high rocks uneventfully, letting the pinto pick its way with caution. There were long hours on the trail, with only the squeaking of saddle leather under his weight, the white fogging of the clear air by the stallion's breath, and an occasional eagle soaring and pirouetting against a cobalt sky.

On the third day out, on the far side of the pass, he stopped at Owens's cabin. Mountain men had an understanding among them that their cabins were available to other trappers when they passed by, whether the owner was in residence or not. So, even when McComb discovered that Owens was not there, he stopped for two nights. He was surprised to find Owens gone, but then remembered Owens telling him, at Bear Lake, that he might go on down to Fort Bridger to sell off the rest of his furs if he did not get rid of all of them at Bear Lake.

That first evening at Owens's small, rather squalid cabin, McComb built a low fire, ate some of Owens's food, and slept in Owens's bed. Then the next day he paid for his visit. He went out into the mountain stream where he knew Owens laid beaver traps, fished the traps out of the cold streams, and retrieved six beavers for Owens. He gutted and skinned them on the sites, and reset the traps in the same places. Then he brought the skins back to the cabin, and hung them up outside for curing. In late afternoon he found a ten-point elk on a high, craggy ridge, and shot it. He placed the carcass on a travois, and the pinto dragged it back to the cabin. McComb cleaned the animal for two hours until sunset, and cut off steaks and chops, and packed the meat in a cooler with ice and snow, to keep it fresh for Owens. He ate none of the meat himself.

McComb left Owens's cabin on the morning of the third day, with the cabin better stocked than it had been on his arrival. He wrote a note to Owens, thanking him for his hospitality, and had the strangest feeling when he finished the note that Owens would never read it. He had never had a thing like that run through his mind before, and it troubled him some. But he figured it was all the result of some bad liquor he had brought along with him, and put it out of his head. One of the things McComb had rejected in the Apache culture was their heavy involvement with superstition and the occult, and he did not like to dwell on matters like this that smacked of unseen forces and dark mysteries.

As McComb rode on out of the South Pass, he came into green meadows and patches of forest, and boulder-spotted mesas thick with jumping cholla and bunchgrass. It was McComb's home territory. He knew every high peak, every stream and river, all of the myriads of gullies and draws that veined the rocky terrain. He knew where every trapper in the area had a headquarters or cabin, was familiar with every turn of every trail that led into and through the pass. Better than all of that, though, he knew where the beavers and ermine lived, and where the bighorns roamed the high buttes, and the locations where he had run onto dangerous cougars or grizzlies on previous occasions. Down on the plains, he knew the migration routes of the buffalo better than most men who specialized in hunting them for their hides.

McComb was looking for a special site now, though. He was seeking out that campsite described to him by Will Beaumont, where Beaumont had found the pendant and comb that McComb knew had belonged to Nalin.

On the second morning out from Owens's cabin, McComb turned onto the secondary trail leading into the pass that Beaumont had told him about. It was not as wide a trail as the big one he had just come off with its myriad wagon tracks and camp-sites, but there was plenty of evidence of the passage of vehicles and animals.

It was about midmorning, with the weather warming up considerably in this lower level, when McComb ran into an unexpected kind of trouble. He rounded a bend in the trail, with rocky outcroppings on his left and a stand of cedars on his right hand, when the bear hove into view.

It was one of the biggest grizzlies McComb had ever seen, and he had seen a few. He wore a permanent scar on his left arm where one had clawed him before he could put a bullet through its brain, in a similar fortuitous encounter.

This one was only fifteen feet away.

The next moments wore a blur of emotional explosions. The pinto, even though a big, strong animal for its breed, panicked immediately, with Mc-Comb trying to hold it steady. But when the ferocious-looking bear hefted its enormous bulk up onto its hind legs, and roared its anger into the morning air, the stallion reared in sudden terror, threw McComb to the ground, and then bolted.

McComb hit the ground hard, wrenching his shoulder as he hit, and saw the pinto gallop off the way it had come, with both of the long guns on its irons.

"Son of a bitch!" McComb gritted out, raising himself up into a sitting position, and feeling his bruised shoulder.

The bear walked a few feet toward him, falling down onto all fours. The big face and jaw, and the angry, small eyes, were a bare eight feet away. It roared again, and the roar echoed through the rocks and trees, and McComb reached for the big Bowie knife on his gun belt. He knew the sidearm would be next to useless now. The big knife came out of its sheath and filled his hand. Its blade glinted in the morning sun.

"By Jesus, you're something!" McComb said breathlessly.

The bear raked at the dirt with its forepaw, and threw gravel onto McComb. He saw the bear was going to charge, and he got onto one knee, the knife ready for use.

"Okay, you beast from hell," he breathed out. "If you want a fight, you've got one."

Almost before the words were out of his mouth, the bear attacked, stepping up over him and raking out with the same claw that had kicked up the dirt. McComb jerked backward, but the claw still ripped across his left shoulder and chest, tearing through the rawhides as if they were paper, and making four ragged wounds across McComb's flesh underneath.

McComb was knocked over, and the bear was on him, grabbing with both of those powerful forelegs, and trying to bite at McComb's head and neck. McComb shoved hard and they rolled over and over together, with McComb trying to keep those razor teeth away from his head. He stabbed at the bear, and hit ribs. The bear came up on top of him, going for his jugular. There was a lot of growling and snarling, and McComb could smell the iron rust smell of the big animal's breath in his face. The bear was digging into his flesh again, on the shoulders and arms, and the big open mouth came down at him again, and the teeth looked a foot long. McComb jabbed upward with all of his strength for the third time, and the silvery blade went home between the bear's ribs.

The bear released its hold on McComb, and McComb jammed the blade in to the hilt, right in the center of the grizzly's massive, furry chest.

The bear coughed, moved off McComb to face away from him, and then fell heavily onto its side, its back leg kicking McComb in the side and almost fracturing a rib.

McComb lay there quietly for a long moment. There were several more grunting sounds from the prone bear, and then it was not breathing anymore. McComb's knife was still in its chest.

McComb found that the kicked rib was all right. His right leg was trapped under the bear's considerable weight, but after a couple attempts, McComb freed it.

He rolled onto his back again, and just lay there breathing hard. He had been unclothed across his chest, and there was plenty of blood. He felt as if he had been run over by a gut wagon.

But no bones were broken, and that was luck. He staggered to his feet unsteadily, and leaned against a nearby sapling. The bear's hind leg moved. McComb drew the Patterson-Colt, aimed at the bear's head just behind the right ear, and fired. The gun roared in the pristine stillness, and the bear jumped a last time, and was still.

McComb holstered the gun, and walked heavily to a creek that ran parallel to the trail off about fifty yards. There he washed the blood off and packed mud into the wounds, Apache style. The wounds were not deep, thanks to McComb's quick reactions. He returned to the trail, and began walking down it in the direction the stallion had run.

It was almost two hours later when McComb finally tracked his horse down. The pinto was standing in a clump of high grass, nibbling at it. It did not shy away when McComb approached it.

McComb made hardship camp only a half mile from the place where the bear had attacked him. He picketed the pinto to a mesquite tree, and threw down a bedroll and made a small fire. Then he further packed his wounds with slick, heavy mud, and wrapped them.

He had a fever through that late afternoon and night, and did not sleep much, and when he did, he dreamed he was under the bear again, wrestling with its great power and weight, and the bear was mauling him, tearing his flesh off his bones, and making a meal of him.

The next morning, the fever was broken. McComb washed the mud off him, and boiled some fat off the grizzly to make a poultice for his wounds. He then put on an extra rawhide shirt, and boarded the stallion, and continued on his way.

He had been delayed in his search for the Gypsy campsite, and he realized that he would not be the same man for a couple of weeks, until the wounds had healed better. He had lost blood, and there would be soreness and stiffness for some time to come. But he had survived. Out here in this raw and pristine wilderness, with its power to crush and maul mere humans in endless ways, survival for just one more day sometimes seemed no mean accomplishment.

He had had a lot of luck.

At the end of that first day after the grizzly confrontation, just as a hooded sun was expiring behind a mauve snow peak in the distant west, McComb found the aging campsite.

Chapter Four

The Gypsy caravan train Yuray Lazlo was with, though, was long gone from the campsite Mc-Comb had found just east of South Pass. Their leader, Antoine Camargue, had made the decision to head west again, toward Fort Bonneville, and although Lazlo was not happy about staying in Mc-Comb country, he went along.

McComb had been right about Nalin being alive, but the Apache girl herself did not think that was any cause for celebration. Since she had been brought to the Gypsies by Lazlo, she had been raped repeatedly, beaten until she had bruises all over her young body, and generally humiliated in endless ways. She was made to perform all of the menial jobs in their camps, and was treated with less respect than the horses that drew the wagons. She was given little food, and what she got were leavings from the Gypsies' plates.

At this point, Nalin wished sometimes that they would just kill her and let it all be over.

Kalderash Gypsies had been in the cities of the

East since colonial days, and in the frontier West for much of that time. They had been distrusted in the East because of their obvious cultural differences, but Westerners had a better reason to keep aloof from them. Renegade bands, such as the one led by Camargue, had a reputation for stealing, deception, and even abduction and murder. A group related by blood to Camargue had stolen so many Apache children to sell off for slavery to enemy tribes that the Apache now killed any Gypsy that came into their territory. And of course that did not motivate Lazlo and the Camargue family to treat Nalin with anything other than hatred and disgust, despite her youth and beauty.

On the day after McComb's discovery of their old campsite, Camargue's group sat around a campfire at sunset, at the base of a rocky butte just a day's ride from Fort Bonneville. They were encircled by four wagons, three they traveled in and a fourth that had been custom-modified as an animal cage, but was now empty. All of them were out there for a serious talk, except for Nalin, who was tied to a wagon stave inside Lazlo's caravan.

The group consisted of Camargue and his wife, an older brother named Ranko, a daughter Kitta and her husband Vaclav Idranyi, and Camargue's younger cousin Lazlo. Playing in the dirt nearby was the overweight and slightly retarded son of Kitta and Idranyi, named Vali.

Antoine Camargue sat on a stool and sucked on a long, handmade pipe. "As I told you weeks ago," he was saying in smooth, well-modulated Romany, "our capital and our supplies are almost gone. As a family business, we are insolvent. There are no other Kalderash in this country, either, to call on for help, and we dare not travel south into Apache territory."

"Did we not resolve to speak always in the native tongue, my brother?" Ranko gently reminded him, sitting opposite Camargue on a low bench with Yuray Lazlo. Ranko was white-haired and wrinkled with age, and had been born in Hungary, as had Camargue and his wife.

Kitta and Idranyi, sitting together on a thick log, exchanged an acid smile. Ranko was considered senile by Camargue, and nobody ever paid any attention to his opinions. But the group now crossed over into English.

"Yes, yes," Camargue said in thickly accented English. "We agreed it is a tool of survival. But survival has more important aspects at this grim moment, brother."

Camargue held his hands out toward the warmth of the flickering fire, and Madame Camargue put a hand lightly on his back. She and her daughter Kitta wore colorful blouses and long ruffled skirts, and gold jewelry hung from their wrists and necks. The men wore dull-looking work shirts and trousers, and Idranyi had a curved knife in a sheath on his belt.

"Then I say it's time to go out and take what we need, wherever we find it," Yuray Lazlo said in his gruff voice. He spoke English without a trace of accent, because he had lived outside the tribe much of his adult life. He was a square-jawed, rather brawny fellow with dark, curly hair and hooded eyes. He had a strong hooked nose and a full mouth and his manner was ordinarily devil-may-care and reckless. But he had sobered of late, when he had heard of Skinner's incarceration and McComb's vow to avenge Nalin and the friend Skinner and Lazlo had killed. At this juncture, however, he had never laid eyes on McComb, and had no idea what he looked like.

Vali came and stood behind his parents, kicking his toe at the dirt, the fire making kaleidoscopic flickerings on his rather surly face. He had been raised to believe that the Marime Code and the Gypsy religion were the only rules necessary to live by, and that non-Gypsies, particularly Indians, were a lesser breed of men. He had observed from his relatives that it was not wrong to steal, deceive, or even take the life of a non-Gypsy.

It was quiet for a moment around the fire, and out in the high rocks somewhere a coyote howled into the encroaching night. The boy looked toward the sound with a frown.

"I hate that sound," Kitta muttered to the fire.

"I have heard Apaches make that call," Ranko commented.

They all looked at him soberly. Kitta pulled a shawl over her slim shoulders, and her mother tugged a babushka tighter under her chin. The

American West would never seem like home to any of them. Lazlo took a stick and lazily stirred the fire up with it.

"Does that mean you have a plan for going and taking what we need?" Idranyi said to Lazlo with a grin. He was Lazlo's height, which was average, but slimmer, and he had rakish good looks, with straight black hair and deep blue eyes. Kitta did not particularly like it that he had begun a kind of camaraderie with Lazlo, since Lazlo's return to the group. Not because of Lazlo's lack of scruples, but because she thought Lazlo was the kind who would get them all into trouble.

"Yuray always has a plan," she said rather sourly. She was rather Italian-looking, with long, auburn hair and fine features, and she was the family's "Little Egypt," the dancer who made the frontiersmen stare in lust when she wiggled her hips in her belly dances.

Both Lazlo and Camargue gave Kitta a sober look. Women were supposed to be seen and not heard at these meetings. An adult woman was a source of pollution to a Gypsy. She must keep her lower body covered to midcalf, sit with legs crossed, avoid stepping over men's clothing. She could not sleep in her husband's bed during menstruation.

"Yes," Lazlo said in an acid voice. "I always have a plan. When I came back to you, you were eating withered turnips three times a day, and your horses were starving. You have had food in your bellies

71

for a year, and it is because I know how to survive."

"You know how to steal," Kitta said with a pleasant smile. She sat closely beside Idranyi, her full skirts gathered between her long legs.

"Enough, Kitta," Madame said to her daughter.

Kitta turned a sour look on Madame. Madame, Camargue, and Ranko had all been poor in Hungary, and had emigrated to America because of tales of riches in the New World. Upon arrival, most Gypsies managed to fit in on the edge of the new society, despite considerable hostility toward them. But some, like Camargue's renegade family, lost any remnant of morality they had brought across the sea with them, and did what they had to, to survive.

"Let us allow Yuray to speak," Madame added.

Kitta sighed heavily under the censure, and looked away from her mother.

"Yes, please go on, Yuray," Camargue told him. He and Ranko fixed their gaze on Lazlo. Camargue was no stranger to chicanery, and he was ready to listen to Lazlo. Ranko had always regretted any act of outlawry the group committed, but his opinion was not respected anymore.

Lazlo grunted in his throat. "Let's get back to doing what we're best at. We can't survive by putting on these fancy shows you did in Europe. This is a hostile land. There are no real towns out here, nobody with money to spend. You don't want to go back East, so I say we make for California. There are people out there starting to find gold in the ground. That's where the money is going to be. Nevada or California. Some say the next decade will see untold riches out there."

"I agree with Yuray, Antoine," Idranyi said. "Survival is just too difficult in this area. You do not get rich trading with the Shoshoni."

"I personally do not have to be rich," Camargue said softly. "But it is important that we survive. Not only as individuals, but as a tribe and a nation within a nation. The Shoshoni and Apache are adapted to this land, but we are not. We must not perish out here."

"But we do not have the means to get to California," Ranko Camargue spoke up, in his weak, old man's voice. "Better we go back to Boston or Richmond, where men are civilized even though hateful toward us. The younger men might find employment there."

"Yes," Lazlo said bitterly. "Shining rich men's boots, and washing their clothes."

"Yuray is right," Idranyi put in forcefully. Kitta gave him a dark sidewise look.

"We can get to California," Lazlo said. "All we have to do is supplement our exhibitions and shows with robbery."

Camargue and Ranko met and held his gaze.

"Exactly," Idranyi said.

"This can be a dangerous pursuit," Madame Camargue said. She was now methodically knitting a shawl on her lap, where she sat next to Camargue on a camp stool. She was a rather handsome

73

woman in her middle age, with dark, sultry features and coal-black eyes that seemed to hypnotize customers who looked into Madame's crystal ball to view their futures.

"Let's rustle horses," Vali blurted out from behind his mother. At fourteen years old, he was a spoiled, bad-tempered youngster who picked his nose a lot and masturbated regularly in the dark corners of the brightly painted, conestogalike caravans that were pulled by two small horses each. He figured that in another year, Lazlo would let him begin fornicating with the Apache squaw Nalin, and he took any opportunity to hide and watch Nalin undress in Lazlo's caravan.

"Be quiet, damn it," Kitta hissed at her rather bulky, oversized, awkward-looking son.

Lazlo grinned at the boy. "Rustling takes a special skill, Vali. No, I think we should concentrate on stealing money, and trade goods. From settlers, miners, ranchers. Vack and me can handle it, the rest of you won't be involved." Kitta hated it when he shortened Vaclav Idranyi's first name to Vack. "But we have to do something." He pointed toward the cage wagon. "The goddamn bear died, and Madame hasn't done any good with fortune-telling out here. People don't seem to worry none about their future. Kitta here only has another few years of dancing until nobody will care to watch her. When we get to California, we could join up with other Kalderash there, and regroup."

Kitta was glaring at him because of the remark

about her losing her figure. She glanced at Idranyi, to see if he would defend her, and he just looked away.

"Maybe you can teach that Apache savage to dance our dances," Kitta said angrily to Lazlo. "She doesn't seem to be good for anything else!"

Lazlo rose with a grin. "That's a matter of opinion, I guess," he said. "Anyway, Vack and me got some ideas, and we'll be telling you more about them. Antoine, I ask permission to be excused." It was a mere formality, but Lazlo knew enough to observe it, as long as Camargue was head of the family.

Camargue liked the deference. "Yes, of course, Yuray," he responded easily.

The meeting broke up shortly after that, and Vali was put to bed by Kitta. The others climbed into their wagons with their painted wood sides and cloth and canvas coverings, and Lazlo found Nalin awake in their caravan, sewing a rawhide jacket she had brought with her upon her abduction because she had been wearing it. She was tied to the wagon with a rope on her ankle.

"How much of that out there did you hear?" Lazlo asked her, when he had seated himself beside her on the blanketed floor of the wagon. He casually reached over and untied her.

Nalin looked up at him warily. She was a raven-haired beauty, wearing a cloth blouse and long skirt given to her by the Gypsies, all very plain and worn clothing. But under the cloth there was a shapely, curved body that had aroused Skinner's and Lazlo's hunger on that day when they came into McComb's cabin like an angry whirlwind.

She spoke good English with a melodic accent. "I do not listen to your talking," she said in the soft voice. She averted her gaze from his. "It does not interest me."

Lazlo grinned. "Does this interest you, little Apache dove?" he said, taking her breast in his grasp and moving his hand on her.

Nalin had learned quickly not to cross Lazlo when he wanted to satisfy his physical appetite. She averted her dark eyes again, and let him have his way. In a moment he was forcing her into a supine position, and had hiked up the long skirt to bare the long, bronze legs. She gasped as he fondled her, and then climbed on her.

While it was happening, she tried to think of Zachariah McComb, and the wonderful days they had had together before these terrible people had come into their lives. She wondered if McComb ever learned what had happened to her, from the one called Skinner, and whether McComb might have lost his life in trying to avenge her.

When she finished remembering and wondering, it was over, and the dark and swarthy Lazlo was lying silent beside her, sated with his lust.

Nalin knew she could not do this forever. She had now given up on McComb ever finding her, and the one last thing available to her was to take her own life. She lay there and thought about that.

Some day or night she would find a knife or gun, and she would do it quickly, and it would be over.

She would join her ancestors in Apache honor, and she would be cleansed of the white man's filth.

At this ugly moment in her life, it was something to consider seriously.

Back in the South Pass area, McComb had spent most of that same morning studying spoor left by the caravan train. He read spoor in the Apache way, patiently and in great detail, and nobody could follow a trail better, white man or Indian.

McComb learned in those three hours that there were four wagons at the encampment, and ten horses. He deduced that eight of the horses were smaller in size and weight, and were probably used to haul the vehicles. The other two were mounts, and were kept for riding. He even knew that one of the wagons was much lighter than the other three, and figured it had some special use other than being a living quarters for the travelers. He saw the tracks of four men, a child, and three women, and one of the women wore moccasins. That would be Nalin, and he now knew there was a good chance that she was still alive.

Actually, McComb had begun reading signs on the trail as he approached the campsite the day before, and now he knew that the Gypsies had gone off in the same direction he himself had just come from, and were on their way through South Pass in a westerly direction.

McComb began reversing direction before noon that day, and spent the entire afternoon following sign and spoor. There were areas where the wagons had passed over sheer rock, and tracks gave out completely, but then McComb would begin a deliberate spiraling outward from the place where he lost the trail, and finally he would find something rather innocuous, like a small dropping from a trace horse, or a grating scratch on a rock, made by the edge of a wheel. In late afternoon, he saw smoke from a campfire up on the trail ahead. He had come back through the pass, and was off the main trail, following the Camargue train, and was not far behind them but he did not know that.

As he approached the campfire, he reined in the pinto and looked into a small stand of pines. There was a wagon and three mounts picketed to it, and three men dressed very much like McComb stood around the fire staring toward him. The wagon was an open one loaded with hides, and McComb recognized the men immediately as buffalo hunters.

The men who specialized in hunting shaggies were newcomers to the frontier, as far as McComb was concerned. The market in the East was just developing for buffalo robes, and as the business grew, it attracted all sorts of men to it, and not all of them were the kind a man would want to ride the trail with. Some found out they were no good at hunting, and turned to outlawry of one kind or another, so McComb had become wary of them as a group.

McComb spurred the pinto and it moved on in to the camp.

The three men watched him ride up. One was big and bulky in his clothing, with a beefy face and one ear missing. He was an ugly man, and looked as hard as sacked wheat. A stringy, skinny man stood up beside him, bareheaded with wild-looking hair, and his eyes were such a light blue that the irises were almost invisible against the whites of his eyes. The third man stood just behind them, on the far side of their small fire. He was short and dumpy-looking, and whereas the first two wore buckskins, this one was bundled up in eastern clothes, topped off with a beaver hat. All three wore sidearms on their belts.

McComb rode up to within fifteen feet of them. He nodded, and spoke to them. "Boys."

The big man with his right ear gone put on a grin that seemed a false one to McComb. "Well, looky here. We got a visit from another shaggy chaser."

The thin fellow tried a grin, too, but it didn't work as well. He had heavy lines around his mouth when he did so, as if his face had shrunk down from a larger size and left a lot of extra skin. "Come on in and get yourself a swallow of chicory, stranger," he said in a rather high, reedy voice.

"Don't mind if I do," McComb responded. He was not wearing the Patterson-Colt revolver, and now felt a little naked without it on. He dismounted and led the pinto to their hide wagon and picketed it there. All three watched him carefully. The short fellow gave the burly one a knowing look.

McComb came over to the fire. "You got some nice robes there."

"We been lucky." One-ear grinned. "You done any good?"

The slim man handed McComb a cup of chicory coffee, and McComb nodded and took it. "I hunt them once a year, when they migrate into my area. Otherwise I pretty much stick to trapping beaver and ermine, up in the high rocks."

"Oh, a mountain man," the skinny fellow said in a different voice. "They say you boys is more Indian than white man."

McComb eyed him studiedly. "I reckon some of us are."

The big, one-eared fellow regarded McComb seriously, and then burst out laughing, as if McComb had said something very funny.

"Where are you headed, mountain man?" the short man with the beaver hat said.

McComb turned to him. He sounded better educated than the other two, and McComb noticed now that his eyes had a more intelligent look to them.

McComb sipped the coffee. "Well, it depends. I'm trailing a Gypsy train that came this way recently. You boys seen anything like that hereabouts?"

"Why, hell, yes," One-ear said in a deep voice. "They can't be a couple hours' ride up the trail, the way you're headed."

The dumpy fellow in the beaver hat gave the big man a hard look, but McComb missed it.

"What you want to find them Gypsies for?" the skinny hunter said, moving up to the fire. He was one of the dirtiest-looking men McComb had ever seen.

Beaver Hat intervened. "Now, that ain't right, Hooker, to ask into a man's business."

McComb sipped some more coffee. "It's all right. I'm looking for an Indian woman they've got with them. Did you happen to see one?"

Beaver Hat shook his head. "We don't talk to no Gypsies. They make my goddamn flesh creep. No, we didn't see who they had with them."

"They're just dressed-up Indians," Hooker offered with a crooked grin.

McComb swigged the rest of the chicory, and tossed some dregs onto the ground beside the fire. He was getting an uneasy feeling about these men, and he had gotten all the information he could from them.

"Well, I appreciate the company, boys. I'll go try to catch that wagon train now."

Beaver Hat took the cup from him. "Hope you find it, mister," he said, and grinned for the first time. McComb nodded, and turned and headed for his mount. Beaver Hat nodded quickly to One-ear, and the big fellow drew a well-oiled revolver from its holster on his hip, and fired it at the back of McComb's head.

McComb heard the movement, and turned slightly as the shot rang out. Instead of entering his skull, the ball of lead glanced off the side of it, and turned on bright-colored lights inside McComb's head, as if a rocket had exploded in there. He was thrown violently to the ground beside the pinto, a low groan issuing from his throat. He lay motionless.

Hooker laughed giddily, and One-ear reholstered his gun. Beaver Hat looked at McComb for a long moment, and then headed toward the hide wagon. "Take everything he's got," he said to Hooker. "Look for money. Get those guns off his mount's irons. We got to make some time if we're going to get to South Pass. You get the horses ready, Sloan."

The big man called Sloan gave him a look. He wanted to search McComb with Hooker. But he went to the wagon as instructed. Hooker went over and looked down at McComb, and giggled quietly.

"He's done for," he said to the others.

He knelt over McComb's chest, and McComb's arm came up like a snake striking, with the hunting knife in his fist, the Bowie he always carried on him, whether he had the revolver or not. The blade sank into Hooker's torso just under the sternum and drove up into his heart.

Hooker's eyes saucered, and he began gasping

and grunting loudly, still kneeling there over Mc-Comb. McComb was afraid he would black out again at any moment, and needles of sharp pain stabbed through his head. He grabbed at Hooker's gun, a Lang double-barreled holster pistol, just as Beaver Hat and Logan turned quizzically toward Hooker.

Deceptively fast for his looks, the small man in the hat drew a revolver, aimed it at McComb, and fired off two quick shots. McComb twisted Hooker's back into the line of fire, and the dying man took both bullets in the back, the body flinching with each hit. McComb aimed carefully and fired the first barrel of the Lang, and there was a sharp explosion, and Beaver Hat was picked up off his feet and hurled against the frame of the hide wagon, crashing loudly there. The picketed mounts began whinnying nervously, and McComb's pinto pulled hard at its picket rope.

Sloan now had his old revolver trained on Mc-Comb, but when he squeezed the trigger, it did not fire. It had misfired on a dud cartridge. He turned in panic and went for a rifle on the irons of the nearest horse. Just as he was pulling it loose from its saddle scabbard, though, McComb fired the second barrel of the Lang.

The sidearm cracked loudly for the second time as Hooker's body fell heavily beside McComb. Sloan grabbed at his back, his big hand clutching spasmodically at the place where the lead had hit him in the middle spine. The shot had cracked a vertebra, dislodged a rib, and burst Sloan's heart like a cactus pear. The mount he fell against broke loose from its tether and galloped off, and the others were rearing and snorting.

McComb fell back onto his back again, breathing heavily, and blackness crowded in on him once more. His Stetson had been knocked off, and his dark hair was disheveled. He put a hand to his head, and felt blood on his hand. It had run down onto his jaw, too, and his neck. He felt very dizzy.

He shoved Hooker's leg off him, and tried to rise. The blackness welled in, and he could not see straight. He sat up, then awkwardly rose to one knee. He grunted heavily in his beard. He wondered if his skull was cracked.

He finally managed to get his feet under him, and sheathed the Bowie after wiping it clean on Hooker's shirt. He started to leave Hooker, then dropped down to one knee again, pulling the Bowie back out. Very methodically he cut Hooker's scalp off and ripped it from his head. He staggered over to Sloan, and did the same thing. He hooked the bloody scalps into his belt. He would let them remind him, later, of possible treachery on the trail. He had done it before, when he had had to kill other men. It was the Apache way, and it was one reason other white men regarded McComb as a savage.

When he was finished with Logan, he went over to the leader, the dumpy man who wore the beaver hat. The hat was on the ground now, and its wearer was very dead, as were the others. Under the hat had been a long shock of red hair, and McComb stared at it now, groggily. Scalping was not enough for this one.

McComb took the bloody Bowie and knelt beside the fallen figure. With one hand he grabbed the head of the dumpy man by the flaming hair, and with the other he cut into the neck of the corpse, through meat and tendon and then bone. In just moments, the head hung in McComb's grasp. He then took a slim rope from his saddle wallet, tied the corpse's hair with it, and then hung the open-eyed corpse up on a nearby limb of a pine tree, at just above head level. It would tell all Indians in the area and some knowledgeable white men that a bad man had died here, and paid for at least one of his wrongs.

When McComb finished, he was very weak. He climbed aboard the pinto, and left the campsite, feeling worse with every moment that passed. Within an hour, and when he was but a short ride of the encamped Camargue train, he blacked out again, fell from the pinto, and lay unconscious on the trail.

In midafternoon that day, Camargue had asked Idranyi and Lazlo to go out with rifles into the surrounding hills and try to shoot them some game.

They had had no more discussion about their future, because Camargue had indicated that he wanted to think it all over by himself before they had another formal meeting.

It was almost dusk when Yuray Lazlo abruptly stopped his mount, a chestnut mustang stallion, and stared ahead on the trail. Vaclav Idranyi came up behind him curiously, a Plains rifle held loosely across his saddle horn. "What is it?" he said.

Lazlo pointed at the figure on the ground, about fifteen yards ahead of them. Not far from it, a horse with saddlery and irons stood and grazed at bunchgrass.

"Looks like a man," Lazlo answered.

They dismounted, and both men stared some more. Idranyi had the rifle in hand, and Lazlo now pulled a Tranter revolver from its holster. They approached the sprawled figure warily.

On the ground, McComb was coming around, but was only half conscious. He moved slightly, and a groan came from the depths of his chest.

They now stood over him. "Well," Lazlo said. "We only shot a rabbit, but look what else we found."

Idranyi grinned his handsome grin. "The pinto has guns on its irons. There may be money."

"Go take a look," Lazlo told him.

Idranyi went over to the pinto stallion, and caught its reins. It guffered a little nervously. He looked at the long guns and went through the saddlebags while Lazlo squatted over McComb. This was the man whose cabin he had ransacked that violent day, and whose friend he and Skinner had

86

killed, and whose Apache woman Lazlo now raped and brutalized every day of her life. But he did not know that. He had never laid eyes on McComb.

"It's one of them hunters," he said to Idranyi. "Probably a buffalo man." They were a long way from McComb's home base, and it did not once occur to Lazlo that this might be the man whose life Skinner and he had so dramatically changed.

Idranyi looked over at him. "There are a few gold coins here. They were hidden in a compartment of the saddle wallet."

Lazlo heard a second groan come from McComb. He reached and looked at the head wound. "Good, we can use that money. Looks like somebody shot this hunter. But he was just creased."

McComb heard the voices, and it was as if they were coming to him from the far end of a long tunnel.

"He might have got back at them, though," Lazlo said with a shaking of his head. "There's a couple of scalps on his belt. He's probably a breed."

"Goddamn savage," Idranyi said, counting the coins as he came back over to Lazlo. "Looks like about fifty dollars here. This will get us some food and supplies."

Just then McComb's eyes fluttered open, and he saw Lazlo squatting over him. In his mind he thought Lazlo was one of the hunters he had just fought with and killed, and suddenly he lashed out at Lazlo, hitting him on the jaw with a right fist.

Lazlo was surprised, and hit the ground beside McComb in a sitting position. He pointed the Tranter at McComb, but McComb fell back on the ground, half conscious. Lazlo rose to his feet, scowling, and touching the bloody place on his lower lip. He aimed the gun at McComb's face. "Son of a bitch!" he swore. "Goddamn wild man!" He kicked out at McComb, and connected with McComb's side. McComb groaned under the impact. Lazlo kicked again, and hit McComb's hip.

"Die, you goddamn wild animal!" Lazlo grated out at the bearded, primitive-looking man lying at his feet. He reaimed the Tranter, figuring to blow McComb's head apart, and squeezed down on the trigger.

Chapter Five

"Wait!" Vaclav Idranyi yelled at Lazlo.

Lazlo released his grip on the trigger of his revolver, and glanced over at Idranyi.

"What?"

"Don't kill him," Idranyi said.

Lazlo gave him a hard look. "Why the hell not?"

Idranyi came up close to Lazlo, and looked down at McComb. "Look at him. Did you ever see a wilder-looking man in all of your life?"

Lazlo lowered the Tranter. "So what?"

"There is a distant cousin of Antoine, the one who is already in California. He owned a wild man until he died."

"Owned?" Lazlo said, becoming interested.

"They had found the fellow raving mad at a deserted mission of the Jesuits. He looked a lot like this man. They kept him in a cage just like our bear cage, and made him perform tricks for the *gaje* at their wagon shows. The longer they had him, the crazier he acted, and the more money they made." He looked down at McComb, and McComb stirred and moaned. "We could do the same thing with this one, since he probably will recover from his wound."

Lazlo thought about that for a moment, and he began liking Idranyi's idea. Once a man is shot, you have no further means of hurting him, as Lazlo wished to hurt this fallen man now. But if you took him captive and caged him, you could take your anger out on him day after day until you were satiated with it. And Idranyi might be right, they might just be able to make money by using this beast-man in their little show, until Lazlo and Idranyi could find them some real money to steal.

He holstered the weapon. "I think you may have come up with a kind of brilliant idea, Vack." He grinned.

"Then let's take him back to the wagons," Idranyi said. "The women will love this."

They were able to bind McComb's wrists and ankles with no further struggle from him, because he lapsed into deep unconsciousness for a while. Together they threw him over his mount, tied him to the saddle, and took him back to their camp that way.

It was dark when they arrived, and Camargue and the others were outside waiting for their return. When Lazlo cut McComb loose from his saddle and dumped him onto the ground near the bear cage wagon, they all gathered around to see what the twosome had brought them. When Idranyi explained, Camargue showed a grin with two teeth missing.

"It could make our show exciting," he agreed. "Very exciting, my son."

"He is a filthy brute," Madame Camargue commented. She wore a long silk dress of old-Europe design, and had a shawl over her shoulders.

Kitta stood beside her. "I like the looks of him." She was a full-breasted, rather voluptuous young woman who excited male appetites when she danced her belly dance for the *gaje*.

Her spoiled son poked McComb with a stick, to see if he would move. McComb did not. Ranko Camargue stood off to one side and scowled. "Where did you find him?" he said in his old-man's voice.

"Not far from here, over toward the pass," Lazlo replied. "Here, Vack, help me with him." He had opened up the door of the cage wagon, on its back end, and they picked McComb up and dumped him inside, on the wood floor that was littered with straw.

"Vali, pull his shirt off," Idranyi said to his son. Vali climbed up into the wagon. "And remove his boots and socks. Maybe we should even cut off his trousers above the knee. We want him to look as uncivilized as possible."

Vali began pulling on McComb's rawhide shirt. McComb did not even know anything was happening to him, although he groaned partway

91

through the procedure, and Vali jumped back slightly, as if he were handling a bear.

"I will cut his trousers off short," Kitta volunteered quietly, and when Idranyi looked toward her, he saw a lust in her dark eyes for the unconscious stranger.

"There is plenty of time for that, my love," he said sourly. "Go prepare the evening meal with Nalin. The sun is long down."

Kitta gave him a defiant look, but turned and left. At that same moment, Nalin came around the corner of the adjacent wagon and squinted into the bear cage where they had placed McComb, and Camargue was holding an oil lantern up near McComb's face, from outside the cage bars. Nalin gasped slightly and her dark eyes went big and round.

"Gods of my ancestors!" she breathed softly in Apache.

Kitta saw the reaction, but misunderstood it. "Come, Indian. You may gawk at the bear-man tomorrow morning. It seems the men do not want us about."

In that moment, Nalin knew that the man in the bear cage was McComb. She glanced quickly at Lazlo, to see if he had noticed her emotional reaction. He had not even known she was there. Nalin swallowed hard, and tried to hide her feelings. It seemed that Lazlo did not know who Mc-Comb was. If Nalin helped Lazlo identify McComb, she would be sealing his death warrant.

92

So she must not show what she knew, in her face. She turned to Kitta. "Yes, Madame Idranyi."

As she joined Kitta, and the boy Vali now yanked at McComb's boots, Ranko came up closer to the cage. "What I was trying to say is that we are in this man's territory. You can't use him in a show in this area. Somebody will surely recognize him."

Idranyi shrugged. "A man like this lives alone. Nobody is likely to know him at a settlement or ranch. Anyway, we will be moving away from the South Pass area soon now, to the west." They had spoken again of California, and decided to make their way to the coast, with Camargue's formal approval.

"This kind of thing is so — unnecessary," Ranko grumbled, turning and leaving them.

Lazlo and Idranyi exchanged a grin. "But so much fun," Lazlo said.

"I think he may bring in some customers," Camargue commented. "My cousin in California featured a beast-man in his show. He draped the wagon with a cloth, and then raised it dramatically after curiosity was aroused to a fever pitch. Of course, he will have to be smeared with dirt, and made to look bestial. As his mind goes, he will be a greater attraction."

Vali had McComb's boots off. "Come on out of there," Idranyi said to him. Vali obeyed. Idranyi went and reached in and cut the bonds on McComb's ankles, but left the ones on his wrists.

Then he closed and locked the cage door.

Lazlo looked into the cage at the unconscious McComb. "Sweet dreams, hunter," he said acidly.

The next morning was clear and balmy. Around the encampment was a straggly stand of red cedar trees, their branches rose-edged with the early sun. The same hue painted the high buttes that soared off to the north of the camp. In the camp itself, the aroma of boiling coffee permeated the air.

In the bear wagon, McComb stirred and groaned and his eyelids fluttered open. He focused and found he could see straight again, and then a deep frown creased his bearded face as he saw the iron bars of the cage he lay in.

"What the hell," he muttered. He tried to move, and found that his hands were tied. Then he realized where he was, seeing the other wagons and the campfire nearby. He could not remember for a moment how he had gotten into this situation, but then it began coming back to him, and the scene with the buffalo hunters formed in his head like a fog was clearing from it.

He moved again, and he hurt all over. But mostly it was his head. Sharp knives of pain sliced through it with any movement, and he recalled being shot. Then he remembered the Gypsies standing over him. They had brought him here and thrown him into this cage.

He managed to hoist himself up against the bars of the cage. He saw that he was half naked and dirty. Kitta and Vali had cut his trousers short, halfway up the thigh, and those short pants were his only clothing. Vali had also smudged him with a stick, from outside the cage, and put char and mud on him to make him look more bestial. All of that, together with McComb's wild dark beard and hair, had accomplished the purpose. McComb felt a couple of itchy places on him, and figured they were lice bites from the matted straw on which he had slept. Over in the corner of the cage lay a thin, wrinkled blanket someone had thrown there for him, but which he had not used.

"Son of a bitch," he said to himself.

Ranko Camargue appeared from a wagon, and walked to the campfire and poured himself some coffee. McComb situated himself so that he could observe the small enclosure made by the formation of the wagons. He narrowed his eyes down on Ranko, and wondered if this was the group he had trailed. He figured it almost had to be, and if so, Nalin might be among these lawless people. Ranko disappeared behind a wagon again, and then McComb saw Nalin.

She appeared quite suddenly from the wagon to the right of his cage, and she immediately saw that he was awake. McComb's look softened when he recognized her. She came over to the cage, and she looked as beautiful as ever to him. But it was clear she had been mistreated.

"My God. Nalin," he said.

She touched a finger to her lips, and whispered to him. "Do not show them you know me, my lover," she said. She came around to his side of the cage, behind him. "I knew you would come for me. Are you badly hurt?"

"I'll be all right," he said. "What the hell is all of this?"

"I heard them talking. They will use you in their shows," she said. "Like a wild animal."

He uttered an Apache obscenity. "What have they done to you, Nalin?"

She averted her eyes for a moment. "I have been — used."

He swore again, angrily.

"No, it is all right, McComb," she said in a whisper. "I survived. I must admit I had almost given up hope, and was thinking dark thoughts. But now it will be all right. We must wait for opportunity, and be patient."

"I'm — so damned sorry, Nalin," McComb said, sighing heavily.

She risked putting a slender hand through the bars, and touching his head lightly. "I am luckier than your friend that they murdered. Now it will be good, if we are careful and do not let them kill us."

They heard a man's voice from the nearby wagon. *"Nalin!"* the gruff voice came. *"Bring me some coffee, damn it!"*

"It is Lazlo, the one who brought me here," she

96

said. "I—sleep in his wagon, McComb." He turned and met her gaze with a hard one. "I must go."

McComb held her look. "Don't talk to me again. Don't even look at me," he told her. "It's too dangerous."

She nodded, and left him.

The morning was bad for McComb. They gave him no food or water, and Madame Camargue and Vali came and laughed at him and called him dirty Gypsy names and poked at him with sharp sticks. If he yelled out his anger at them, Madame would spit on him. Lazlo loved all of it. At one point he brought Nalin over to see the caged wild man, and it was a tense moment for her. But she put on a good act, and appeared disgusted with the sight of him.

"Look at that." Lazlo laughed, turning to Idranyi near him. "Even a goddamn Indian can't stand the sight of him. I tell you, we got us a gold mine here."

"What did I say to you?" Idranyi replied. "Didn't I promise you this is better than killing him?"

Nalin was allowed to leave, and just Lazlo and Idranyi stood by the cage. McComb eyed them with predatory hostility. If the opportunity arose to kill either of these men, he would not make death easy for them.

"What do you think of that, wild man?" Lazlo grinned at McComb. "You want to earn your keep by putting on a wild-man show for the paying customers, next time we get to civilization?"

McComb glared sullenly at him, through the matted beard. Now he also had shallow wounds in his chest, side and back, from the stabbing with sharp sticks. Vali enjoyed hurting anything that was helpless.

"I don't think he talks," Idranyi put in. "That's all the better. Don't you know even a few words of human speech, wild man?"

McComb met his gaze with a brittle one. "The stink here is worse than a buffalo camp," he said in his deep voice.

Their faces changed, and the grins evaporated like dew on prairie grass. A scowl grew on Idranyi's handsome face. "Stink?" he said emotionally. "An animal like you talks of stink in my camp, you sorry-looking son of a bitch?"

Lazlo came up to the bars. "God, am I glad I didn't kill you, you goddamn hill hermit. Whose scalps did you have on your belt when we found you? What did you do to them, maybe eat them? What brand of Indian savage have you got in them veins of yours?"

"Why don't you go play with yourself, Gypsy?" McComb grunted out from his throat.

Lazlo's face colored slightly, and hot anger showed in it. But then he realized that McComb was totally in his power, and the future was owned by himself, Lazlo. He cooled down some. "I guess you don't like eating much." He breathed irregularly. "Because that just cost you two days without food or water, wild man. What do you think of that?"

"I think you'd like pulling wings off of bluebottle flies," McComb said evenly.

Lazlo and Idranyi exchanged a look, and then Lazlo burst out laughing, liking McComb's situation better than any since Emmett Skinner had given Nalin to him.

"Just keep talking, wild man," he said. "You'll wear out soon enough. Then I'll be in that cage with you regular, and we'll have us some real fun." He and Idranyi both had a laugh at that remark, and then they went to eat their morning meal.

At just before noontime, the Gypsies pulled up stakes and set out for Fort Bonneville. McComb had been given nothing to eat or drink, and it was clear that Lazlo would make good on his threat to make him go without. The day turned hot as they came closer to the settlement, and the sun blistered down on McComb's exposed flesh and burned it. He bumped around in the cage badly, and sustained new bruises. But his head was slowly healing, and so were the shallow flesh wounds put there by the Gypsies, and the bear.

It was a long afternoon, but finally the caravan train arrived at Fort Bonneville. It was a settlement similar in looks to Fort Bridger, where Emmett Skinner had intimidated locals and inquired about McComb. The Gypsies made camp out away from the settlement several hundred yards, because no western settlement would allow Gypsies within their boundaries except for one or two at a time, like Indians. Also, no inn would put up a Gypsy for the night.

They encamped under the shade of plane trees, and McComb was glad to be out of the sun at last. His throat was parched from the heat and lack of water, and he was dehydrating fast. Idranyi went into the fort and spread the word that they would be putting on a show that evening. There had not been much excitement in the area since the locals had returned from the trade fair earlier, so there was quite a lot of interest in the announced "Show and Exhibition." Hand-printed flyers told of Madame Camargue's fortune-telling and crystal ball gazing, Idranyi's mystical tricks and supernatural powers, Kitta's sensual dance under the name of Little Egypt, and the brand new Wild Man of Purgatory act, in which a human being raised with animals performed like a bear.

It was also announced that throughout this marvelous show, Camargue himself would sell wondrous nostrums and emetics, mixed to exact perfection and designed to cure a wide spectrum of ills, and even improve sexual performance.

Nalin stayed away from McComb, but it was difficult. She knew the privation and misery he was going through, and how easy it would be for her to slip him a tin cup of water or a scrap of bread. But McComb had given her strict orders to keep away, and she knew he was right. It was very dangerous. If Lazlo even remotely suspected that this was the man who had caught and jailed his ex-partner Skinner, he would undoubtedly kill him immediately. Then he would make Nalin pay dearly for keeping McComb's identity a secret.

At dusk, though, just as the sun was disappearing behind rounded hills in the west, Ranko came to McComb with a small cup of broth. He had just arrived at the cage wagon, when Lazlo spotted him and saw what he was carrying. He came over to Ranko quickly.

"What the hell do you think you're doing?" he said roughly to the old man.

"This nonsense has gone far enough," Ranko said. "If you deprive him of water, he will die."

"To hell with that," Lazlo said. "Let me decide when he's dying."

At the campfire, Kitta and Madame glanced toward the scene. Camargue was inside a wagon, out of sight, as was Nalin. The boy Vali came over to listen to the exchange, and so did his father, Idranyi.

"Now just get the hell out of here, old fool," Lazlo was saying to Ranko.

Idranyi narrowed his eyes slightly on Lazlo. "Easy, my friend. You are talking to a Camargue."

"Let him die," Vali said. "As long as it's slow."

Both men ignored him. Lazlo turned to Idranyi, surprised by the remark. Ranko slipped the broth in between the bars, defying Lazlo. Lazlo saw it, and started to say something, but instead turned back to Idranyi. "What's the matter with you?"

Idranyi sighed. McComb inched over and grabbed the cup with his tied hands, and put it to his mouth, and drank hungrily, a lot of it spilling down onto his naked, muscular chest. Ranko moved off, grunting.

"Ranko is right this time," Idranyi said to Lazlo. "We don't want him sickly, Yuray. He won't make as good an exhibition for us."

Lazlo cooled down. "I don't care how much interest he draws."

"Well, my father-in-law does, I assure you," Idranyi replied. "He places much importance on our exhibitions."

Lazlo turned away from the cage, not wanting to see McComb down the broth. "You and I should be in town cleaning out some purses while the silliness of the show goes on," he said angrily. "We're not going to get to California putting on freak shows and selling nostrums."

"Antoine believes it would be dangerous to do any stealing here," Idranyi reminded Lazlo. "They have a kind of marshal here, a peace officer. We would not be able to escape their wrath if they suspected us in a theft. It is wise to wait until we are farther west, and are passing smaller settlements, and ranches. Then we will work your plan."

Lazlo gave him a look. "Don't make me wait

too long, Vack. I'm getting bored with all of this."
He then turned and walked away.

McComb had drunk all of the broth, and felt a little better. He sat there and watched the two men disperse, and darkness crawl over the campsite. Maybe with the old man there, he might get some strength back, after all. He had examined and tested the cage bars, and the door at the rear of the contraption, and there appeared to be no easy way out. He would need all of his strength and clearness of head to find a way out of this for Nalin and himself. He knew they were camped outside Fort Bonneville, and he knew a couple of traders there. If they came to the show the Gypsies were putting on, somebody might recognize McComb, and do something to help him. Of course, that could be dangerous, too, he knew.

After their supper that evening, the Gypsies prepared for the show. The gaily painted *vardos* that resembled in part the conestogas of the frontier were opened up by letting one side down on the campsite side of the wagon, and that wooden side became a platform on which the various parts of the exhibition-show were enacted. One was a small stage for Kitta, another the same thing for Camargue's pitch show with the patent medicines. A tent was pitched at one side of the large enclosure, and Madame Camargue held court inside it on show nights, sitting at a table which displayed a large crystal ball into which Madame gazed to see the future of paying customers. She also read palms and craniums.

Ranko furnished the music for the show, because he was still very good with the violin. He would sit on a stool in the background, and play music that was exotic to the ear of the western frontiersman, and it was Ranko's music that Kitta danced to, in her part of the entertainment.

Lazlo and Idranyi distributed printed flyers in the settlement, and by dark people began coming. A canvas cover had been hung over the cage wagon, and McComb could not see anything, but he could hear voices out there, and then Camargue trying to sell his nostrums, and shortly thereafter the music that accompanied Kitta's dance.

Out in the compound, Kitta gave a sensual performance for the traders and cowboys, and they loved it. They yelled for more when her dance was finished, and one cowboy tried to grab her ankle to pull her off the small stage. She slapped his face and everybody laughed.

Soon the time came for showing McComb, and when he least expected it, the canvas was pulled off the wagon and McComb was staring into the faces of men and women from the settlement.

McComb was something to look at. Some of the women gasped audibly at the sight of him. Half naked, he was dirt-smeared from the poking with sticks, and straw clung to his body and hair, and his beard and unkempt appearance made him look more like an animal than a human being. He sat hunched all together in the center of the cage, scowling out at them, looking for a familiar face. There was none.

Lazlo stood outside the cage, grinning at McComb. "Here, folks, grab yourself a stick to poke at the Bear Man. Watch him jump and make funny sounds. Raised in a bear's litter, folks. Didn't know how to talk when we got him. Just made crazy grunting sounds. Now, don't get your hands in there, boys, he might just bite one off. When we found him, he'd just killed a Bible drummer and was busy eating the poor fellow's left leg."

More gasping from the few women present.

"I'll be goddamned!" a middle-aged trader exclaimed with a somber look.

Lazlo had passed some sticks around, and now a young man came up to the cage tentatively and thrust it in at McComb, prodding him in the thigh. McComb was weak and groggy, and had not seen it coming. But when the stick punched at his flesh, a quick anger rose in him, and he grabbed the stick violently, making a growling sound in his throat that made Lazlo's story more believable. He yanked the stick from the young trader's hand, broke it savagely in half, and hurled the pieces through the bars at his assailant.

People shrank away from the cage, and thrills of delicious excitement rippled through the insides of the women present.

"Don't do that!" McComb growled out slowly.

Lazlo quickly intervened. "Three of the few

words he knows," he quickly put in. He and Idranyi had warned McComb that if he spoke to the paying customers at a show, they would kill him that same night, and McComb believed them. But his concern with his own mortality had its limits. Idranyi now appeared beside Lazlo, and they were both scowling at him meaningfully.

McComb looked past them, into the compound formed by the wagons. Madame was in her tent, telling a fortune, and Camargue was explaining to a trader how an emetic would cure his ills. The elderly Ranko, violin in hand, stood at the rear of the small crowd, and scowled at the goings-on. It was clear to McComb that he did not think you should treat another human being like this.

"Don't let him scare you," Idranyi was saying to the gathering of about twenty persons. "Those bars are strong, I promise you. He can't hurt you if you use the sticks."

McComb glared silently at Idranyi and Lazlo. A couple more sticks were thrust at him, by young men, and one broke the skin on his back. Again, McComb grabbed at the weapon, but this time he missed, and the crowd had a good laugh. He looked around at their faces, and realized that these were just your ordinary folks, good family people mostly. But few if any thought there was anything wrong with what was happening here.

Lazlo, disappointed with McComb's performance, and concerned somewhat that McComb would continue to cooperate, even to stay alive, finally drew the canvas down on the compound side of the cage, and Idranyi drew the crowd over to view a second dance by Kitta.

McComb hunched into himself, and shook his head. He had seen a Gypsy show a year ago at a trade fair that featured the pickled head of a dead outlaw, and a young Gypsy woman that handled rattlesnakes. But he had never seen any of them use a white man like they were now. He could only imagine the things they had done to Nalin.

"Hey, you."

McComb looked up quickly and saw the skinny, drunken trader that had come around the back side of the cage to get a last look at McComb. McComb glared at him.

"Bear Man, you look like somebody I seen at the Green River Trade Fair a little while ago." His voice was heavily slurred, and he staggered and leaned up against the corner of the wagon.

McComb's eyes narrowed down, and he moved over toward the fellow. "I was there," he said deliberately.

"I can't remember for sure. Might have been down at Bridger. I almost recall—this fellow's name you look like." He was not listening to McComb.

McComb came very close to the bars, and glanced past the man to see if Idranyi or Lazlo were nearby. "Listen to me, damn it!" he hissed out at the fellow. "I was at the fair. I'm a trapper. My name is McComb."

The man did not appear surprised to hear McComb talking. "No, that ain't it."

McComb swore under his breath. The man was hanging his head down, as if he were going to collapse at any moment. McComb whispered harshly to him. "McComb. They abducted me, and put me in this cage. Tell the marshal."

The fellow looked up at him, and saw two McCombs. "You talk—pretty good for a bear." He then turned away, and vomited on the ground beside the wagon.

"Oh, shit," McComb mumbled.

The man staggered away, and McComb realized he would not remember any of this. He slumped back against the end wall of the cage, and there was applause for Kitta's second show, and then he heard the crowd dispersing, getting on mounts and into carriages. A few moments later, he heard two voices near the wagon, and it was Lazlo and Idranyi.

"I'm telling you, he was sure," came the voice of Yuray Lazlo. "Mule is out."

McComb's interest quickened, and he strained to hear.

"How could he know?" Idranyi was responding. "What is his source?"

"It was an express rider that told him," Lazlo said. "It's all over the Devil's Hole area. Skinner busted out and they think he's headed this way." There was excitement in his voice. "If he finds out we're in this area, he'll come to join us, I know it."

There was a long silence, while McComb strained to hear.

"Is this such a good thing, Yuray? I mean, with the law out to take Skinner back?"

Now there was impatience in Lazlo's voice. "Listen to me, Vack. There's no law around here that Skinner can't handle. And the farther west we go, the less law there will be. Mule had some great ideas before the law caught him, Vack. If he finds us, we won't need this cousin of mine. We won't have to grub for pennies in the pockets of dirt poor cowboys. The three of us could split from Antoine, and make some real money."

A briefer silence this time. "I have to admit, it sounds better than this," Idranyi's voice came to McComb.

After that, the two men drifted away, and McComb could not hear them anymore. He hunched into himself there in the darkness of the cage, and absorbed what he had just heard. Nothing could have depressed McComb more than the thought of the escaped Skinner coming to join this Gypsy train. If that happened, McComb's hope of freeing Nalin from these soulless outcasts would be gone, and they both would be as good as dead.

Things were going from bad to worse.

Chapter Six

The diligent search Emmett "Mule" Skinner had made for McComb had so far turned up next to nothing. Not understanding that Skinner was out to kill McComb, traders and trappers had honestly tried to give Skinner some legitimate clues as to where McComb might be, but they were all wrong in their guesses. None of them knew that McComb had heard about the Gypsy troupe, and was out searching for his woman Nalin. So Skinner went off in several directions on those spring days, while McComb was trailing the Gypsies, and just missed crossing their trails a couple of times. Now, down south of Fort Bonneville where Camargue and his group were encamped, Skinner had just heard of their presence at the settlement, and had decided, as Lazlo had guessed, to find them. Skinner rightly guessed that Lazlo would still be with them, and he figured on enlisting Lazlo's aid in locating the mountain man and killing him. Then he and Lazlo could take up where they had left off before McComb had put Skinner behind bars.

The dun mare that Skinner had stolen before his arrival at Fort Bridger had gone lame on him, but he rode the animal, anyway, heaping physical and verbal abuse on the poor beast for days. He was particularly pleased, therefore, when he came upon a lone fur broker camped on a low hill north of Bear Lake, on the day after McComb had been exhibited in the cage, up at Bonneville.

Skinner rode up to the small camp with his mare limping badly. He was dressed in stolen clothing that ill-fitted him, and a dusty looking Stetson covered his bald head. The stolen Derringer revolver was slung low on his right hip.

Skinner studied the scene before him. The trader had not seen him yet, and was squatting beside a low fire. Near the fire also were a hide wagon with a dray horse in harness, and a mount gigged to the rear of the wagon. Skinner studied the mount. It was a sizable, rather sleek Arabian mare, and Skinner's mouth curled upward slightly at the corner when he saw it. He also noted with interest the furs and hides aboard the wagon, and the fine look of the clothing worn by the squatting man. Something stirred malevolently inside Skinner, a predatory something that now anticipated with raw excitement the potential ravaging of a prey.

He rode on into the camp, and the man at the fire turned to look at him, then rose and stood warily.

Skinner put him at ease. "Good day to you, stranger. My mount's pulled up lame on me. Mind if I rest her at your fire?"

111

The other man's face relaxed some. He was young, thin, and well dressed in eastern pants, shirt, and jacket. He did not wear a gun. "No, it's all right," he replied. "Take your weight off the mare for a spell."

Skinner dismounted, and picketed the mare to a nearby shrub. It guffered with relief, and held its right front hoof off the ground slightly.

"Goddamn gimp horse," Skinner grumbled, coming over to the other fellow.

The trader's eyes narrowed slightly at the remark. He pointed at the fire. "As you can see, I got some coffee on. If you want to wait till it boils, you're welcome to a cup."

Skinner nodded. He stood several inches taller than the trader, who looked like a boy next to him. "Might just take you up on that. I had a hard ride." He glanced over at the Arabian, and it was suddenly as nervous as a cow in with a herd of bulls.

The trader glanced at the Derringer on Skinner's hip. "You ride up from Bridger?"

Skinner gave him a look. You did not ask a man's business out here. This fellow did not know that yet, so he was what was called a greenhorn. That made it even easier.

"Oh, I just been wandering in the hills," Skinner told him. "Riding down a break all day, keeping out of a crosswind. Looking for a man."

The trader's eyebrows shot upward. "Oh?"

"A trapper named McComb," Skinner said slowly. He squatted down and held his hands out to the fire. He looked over at the knee-hobbled dray, and then at the bundles of beaver hides on the front of the wagon. On the back part of it were stacked some fine-looking buffalo robes. He guessed, also, that under the buckboard was a box or saddle wallet with money and valuables.

"McComb," the young man said. He had premature lines around his mouth and eyes, and a sharp, angular nose. He wore a rather small beaver hat pushed back slightly on his head. "Ain't he that trapper from South Pass?"

Skinner nodded. "You run into him lately?"

"Never done no business with him at all," the trader said.

Skinner studied his face. "You come from the north?"

"Yeah, been up at Fort Bonneville."

"Run into any Gypsies up there?"

"No, but I heard tell there was a bunch of them camped just to the east of the settlement," the young fellow said. "A family with a funny name. Camargue, I think."

Skinner looked past the trader for a moment. He would probably find Yuray Lazlo with Camargue, he figured. That was good news. Lazlo could help him find and kill McComb. And then they could go back to raising some hell together.

"You could probably catch them there," the trader said.

Skinner eyed him. "What makes you think I'm heading that way?"

The young man was flustered. "Why, I just thought —"

"You're about as brash as a flour peddler running for governor," Skinner said in a new, hard voice. He walked over to the wagon, and ran his hand over a stack of beaver pelts. The trader watched him warily.

"I can sell you some nice furs, if you're in the market," he said to Skinner.

He watched Skinner walk along the side of the wagon, eyeing the furs and robes.

"I could probably give you a special price on some of that stuff, so I wouldn't have to haul it to Bridger."

Skinner did not reply, nor even look at him. He finally went to the dray animal and looked it over contemptuously. "What do you think these hides will bring at Bridger?" he said with nonchalance.

The young man frowned. "Why, I hadn't figured it. Not a total, that is. You thinking of buying the whole lot?" His face now showed concern.

Skinner leaned on the dray horse and grinned slightly at him. "I think I could probably get as good a price for this lot as you, if I took it to Bonneville."

The trader did not like the sound of Skinner's voice now. "I — suppose that's possible. What are you getting at, mister?"

Skinner sighed as if explaining to a child. "What I mean is, boy, that I'm going to sell this stuff at Bonneville."

The trader swallowed back a sudden fear, but pretended he did not understand. "I reckon that would depend if you can meet my price here," he said quietly.

Skinner shook his beefy head. "No, it don't," he corrected the young man. "I ain't paying you nothing for this stuff, boy."

The trader stood there.

"I'm taking your hides, and your animals, and your wagon, and whatever else you got stashed away here." He drew the revolver on his hip and aimed it in the general direction of the other man.

The trader suddenly began trembling. His mouth went dry, and his palms began to feel damp and cold. He had never run onto a bushwhacker before, and had thought the stories of robberies out on the trail were exaggerated.

"Look, mister," he said, licking his lips so he could speak. "Take the stuff. Take the animals. You don't have to use that gun. I'm not going to give you no hard time."

"Hard time?" Skinner said, feigning surprise in his ruddy face. He laughed gutturally. "Boy, if your brains was dynamite, you couldn't blow the top of your head off. How do you think you might give me a hard time?"

The trader swallowed hard. "Just take the stuff, mister," he said, his voice breaking. "It's yours."

"Oh, I know it's mine," Skinner said. "I knew it was mine when I rode up here. You got a shovel in all that wagon equipment?"

"Why, yes. I have."

"You go get that shovel, will you?" Skinner said.

The young man hesitated, then went to the wagon and unstrapped a short-handled shovel from its far side. He came back around and stood there, holding the shovel.

"Now you go over by that granjeno, and dig a hole," Skinner said to him.

The other man glanced toward the shrubs. "Why?"

Skinner sighed, then walked over and swung the barrel of the Derringer Navy revolver up against the side of the younger man's head. It smacked hard there, just over the left ear, and the trader went down. His hat flew off, and he lost the shovel.

Skinner stood over him. He reholstered the revolver. He would not need it. He dropped a brittle look on the supine trader, who was bleeding at the side of his head, and breathing hard.

"Your head must be empty as last year's bird's nest with the bottom punched out," Skinner growled at him.

"Look, mister—" the trader gasped out feebly.

"Get on your feet, and get that hole dug. Six long, three wide," Skinner said slowly.

The other man complied, staggering to his feet and going over beside the bushes that Skinner had indicated. He began digging in the sandy soil there, throwing dirt half-heartedly, his gut tightening inside him. He was digging his own grave, and knew it.

Skinner came and leaned against a nearby cottonwood sapling, and took out makings and rolled up a smoke while the trader bent to his task. Skinner was relaxed, as if he were in a pool hall watching a player try to run the table.

"You got a daddy, boy?" he said, scratching a match on his pants and lighting the brown cigarette.

The young man looked up at him. "Yes."

"Keep digging," Skinner said easily. The trader obeyed.

"What kind of man is he?" Skinner said.

The other man kept digging. "He owns a shoe store back in Ohio."

"Ohio," Skinner said. He took his hat off for a moment and ran a hand over his bald head. "Seems like all the dandies come from Ohio."

The trader dug listlessly. He did not want the job to be finished.

"My daddy come from Georgia," Skinner said while the other man dug. "Back there they called him white trash. He was a real drinker, my daddy. Used to come home with a bellyful, and beat the hell out of me. For nothing."

The trader glanced over at him. If Skinner talked enough, he might change his mind about killing him.

"He was big, bigger than me," Skinner went on, talking more to himself than to the other man. "He'd beat on me till I couldn't walk the next day." A long silence while he remembered. "Then one night I found him dead drunk and asleep."

The trader had made a grave-size hole now, and began to deepen it. He watched Skinner furtively as he dug.

"We had this half-size axe," Skinner went on. "Used it to butcher chickens and hogs. I went and got it, and came into Daddy's room with it. He was just laying there snoring. Snoring so loud it would wake up the dead. Flat on his back."

Skinner replaced the hat to his head, and his eyes narrowed down in pensiveness. "I stood right over him, and raised that axe just like I had a chicken on a block. It had a real sharp blade. When it come down, it just separated his head from his shoulders."

The trader stopped digging, and stared in horror toward Skinner. He was trembling visibly now. He remembered, and went back to digging.

"I'll never forget how clean that blade took his head off," Skinner said. "Of course, blood was everywhere. It come up and hit me in the face, can you imagine that? And through all of that, my daddy's face was alive. I mean, the eyes popped open, and he made some awful faces, and he looked right at me. With his head clean off his body. You never seen nothing like it."

A shudder passed through the trader's chest, and he stopped shoveling, and turned and threw up into the hole. Skinner looked at him quizzically, then went over to him.

"What the hell you doing, boy? You been chewing peyote?"

The trader turned back to him. His face was gray-hued, and a stench arose from the hole. "Mister," he gasped. "I don't know—your name. I won't blow on you."

Skinner grinned. "Somehow I don't give that credence. A trader that will keep his word is as hard to find as a banker in heaven, my boy." He looked into the hole. "Well, that's just about deep enough, I reckon. Now you just lay down in there for me, will you?"

The trader was jerking violently now. "Please."

Skinner frowned. "Get in there, boy," he growled.

The trader hesitated, then got into the hole and lay down in the vomit, on his back.

"Now cross your arms on your chest," Skinner said.

The young man obeyed again.

"Now close your eyes, and you won't know when it's coming," Skinner said to him.

The trader closed his eyes, and lay there trembling. He began mumbling to himself then. "For God so loved the world that he gave His only begotten son, in order that anyone having faith in Him might not be destroyed but have everlasting life."

Skinner looked at him quizzically. He had been going to humiliate and scare the trader, and then let him live. Drive the wagon off with the trader in the grave, and have a big laugh from it. He started away, but heard the trader continue, eyes closed.

"It is written that any who call upon the name of Jehovah shall be saved. For He came to give His soul in ransom for the souls of many."

Something changed inside Skinner, as he heard the words rise to him from the hole, something he did not even understand himself. A desire rose in him, a dark hunger that wanted satiation. In the history of the world, there had never been so submissive a victim, such a desirable recipient of violence as that man in the hole, mouthing words that aroused wild feelings in Skinner.

"Oh, shit," he muttered. He drew the revolver and aimed it at the corpselike figure and squeezed the trigger. There was a loud explosion, and the trader jumped in the hole, and his eyes popped wide open, just as Skinner's father's had. Then Skinner fired three more times, in rapid succession, and when he was finished, he was quite breathless, with little thrills of pleasure skittering through his insides. The trader lay in the hole bloody and lifeless, and Skinner saw his father's face down there, and then it was replaced by that of McComb.

He finally reholstered the revolver, and walked over to his mount and gigged it to the rear end of the wagon, beside the Arabian mare. Then he unpicketed the dray horse and climbed aboard the wagon.

He would drive up to Fort Bonneville, sell off the hides and the wagon, and keep the Arabian as his mount. Then he would join up with Lazlo again, and they would go hunting together.

McComb could not be far off.

It was just a matter of time.

Later that same day, at Camargue's encampment outside Fort Bonneville, Nalin came to McComb just after dusk, against his orders. Lazlo was still starving McComb, and Nalin realized she must get some food to him or he would weaken and become sick. After bringing McComb the broth, the old fellow Ranko had not risked Lazlo's wrath by bringing him any more food. So Nalin figured it was up to her.

It was just getting dark when Nalin appeared at the bear cage with a small loaf of unleavened bread, and a cup of water. The canvas cover over the wagon had been raised on the compound side of the encampment, and McComb could see the Gypsies as they moved about camp. When Nalin came to him, everybody was inside the wagons, resting after the evening meal. They had left Nalin outside to clean up, but she was hobbled with a chain between her ankles. Lazlo did not want her to try to escape.

McComb squinted down hard on her when she arrived at the cage. He knew there was to be no show this evening, since Camargue figured they had gotten all they could from the locals. He planned on resting here for a couple more days, and then heading on farther west, as Lazlo had suggested they should.

"Nalin!" McComb whispered harshly to her, when he saw her at the bars. "I told you. Keep away from me."

"I can't, McComb," she said tearfully. "I can't see you like this. Here." She gave him the bread. "And drink this water."

McComb could not turn down the offer, the water looked too good to him. He looked quickly across the dark compound, then took the cup and guzzled the water quickly. Some ran down his chin. He breathed heavily after drinking. He picked up the bread, hid it behind him, and handed the cup back to her.

"Thanks, Nalin." He looked at her. "I—been missing you."

She brushed at a tear. Indian women were not supposed to show emotion. But she had lived with McComb too long. She could not help herself. "I love you, Zach McComb. We will get free of this. Together. I feel it."

He nodded. He looked very wild to her. "I know. Now, get back to your wagon. This is very dangerous."

"It is even worse, with you here," she said quietly. "Sleeping on his pallet. Letting him touch me."

He shook his head sidewise. "Don't talk about it, Nalin. You lasted this long. Just bide your time. Something will happen, some opportunity will come to us. Be patient."

"All right, McComb. I will try to think of you when—"

She cut her farewell off short when she heard the footstep behind her, and when she whirled around, Yuray Lazlo was standing there. Nalin let out a small cry.

"Well, well," Lazlo said. He came around where McComb could see him, as he grabbed Nalin's wrist. He stared hard into the cage, looking closely at McComb. "So that's it. You're that McComb fellow."

"No, you're wrong!" Nalin protested feebly.

Lazlo grinned. "Forget it, my little Apache bird. I heard you say his name."

Nalin caught McComb's eye. "The gods are angry with me because I disobeyed your orders."

"It's all right, Nalin," McComb said heavily, meeting Lazlo's excited stare.

"I'll be damned," Lazlo said in his throat. "The hunter that owns that cabin in the mountains. Whose friend Skinner killed. Whose woman I sleep with."

McComb just stared at him.

"Let him go!" Nalin said pleadingly. "Let us go. I appeal to your humanity!"

Lazlo glanced at her, and back at McComb, and a grin crept onto his square-jawed face and into his hooded eyes. He grabbed Nalin by the waist, and pulled her to him, grinning at McComb.

"Well, ain't this nice," he said. "I never thought I'd see the day. You had yourself a real piece of woman here, hunter. I want to thank you for breaking her in for me."

"You son of a bitch," McComb growled.

Lazlo laughed in his throat. "Maybe you and me can compare notes on her, McComb. Did you like those hard little bronze breasts? Is she real quiet when you're on her, like she is with me? Did you find out how good she is with her mouth? Or maybe you never even tried that, huh?"

McComb slammed his hand against the bars. "You black-hearted bastard!" His wrists had been freed, for the show they had had.

Nalin struggled loose from Lazlo, and stumbled

123

and fell to the ground near him, and he laughed again.

But when he turned back to the darkened cage, with McComb's wild-looking face just behind the bars, his own face grew somber. "I bet you been tracking us, ain't you? To get the little woman back? Or maybe kill me, too?"

McComb just glared hard at him.

"Well, that just shows you, how things can turn around on you. You hunt us, and we end up putting you in a cage. Funny how things work out, ain't it?"

Nalin got to her feet. "Please, let us go!"

"Let you go? Why, what an idea, little Apache," Lazlo said. "No, I got to kill this man now. He's much too dangerous to have around, you see."

"Oh, no!" Nalin cried out.

"And then I got to kill you," Lazlo said soberly.

McComb let a hissing growl issue from the depths of his chest, and flung himself at the bars, reaching between them with muscular arms to grab at Lazlo's neck. He reached Lazlo with his right hand, and tore at his shirt before Lazlo pulled away and out of reach. Little needles of fear prickled along Lazlo's spine, even after he was out of danger from the wild man. He pulled his Tranter revolver from the holster he still wore on his hip, and aimed it at McComb's face. He was breathing hard, and his eyes were glittery in the darkness.

"I ought to fill you full of lead right now," he said in a harsh, uncertain voice. "But Camargue will want to authorize your execution."

124

McComb sat back on the cage floor, getting himself under control. "She's no more danger to you now than she ever was. You don't have to kill her."

Lazlo grinned. "I might just kill her first, McComb. So you can watch her die."

Just at that moment, the sound of hoofbeats came to them, and a moment later Idranyi rode into camp. He had been into Fort Bonneville to get some supplies. They were strapped to the flanks of the horse he rode. He dismounted, seeing Lazlo over at the cage. Camargue came out from his wagon, and also Kitta. They saw Lazlo and Nalin at the cage, too. They greeted Idranyi, and then the three of them came over to Lazlo and Nalin.

"What is happening?" Idranyi asked Lazlo, seeing Nalin's tear-streaked face.

Lazlo grunted in his throat. "It seems my Indian and the wild man have been keeping a secret from us. They know each other. This is Zach McComb."

Idranyi frowned. "The trapper you stole this girl from?"

"That's right," Lazlo said.

"Oh, hell," Idranyi muttered.

Camargue narrowed his dark eyes, and peered into the cage. Kitta made a sound in her throat to show mild surprise. "Interesting," she mused.

"I knew the girl would bring trouble to us," Camargue was saying. "I felt it."

"You call this trouble?" Lazlo said. "This isn't trouble, Antoine. Give me your permission, and I'll end the trouble tonight. Personally." He touched the gun he had reholstered.

125

Camargue raised his voice. "This man hunts and traps in this area. He must do business at settlements like Fort Bonneville. Someone may have recognized him already, at our show."

"That is true, Yuray," Idranyi put in.

"To hell with that," Lazlo said. "Nobody recognized McComb, if they had, we would know. I say, kill him. Now. And the Apache, too."

Kitta looked at Lazlo, wondering how he could talk of killing Nalin so casually, after living with her and making love to her.

"I must sleep on this," Camargue finally said. "I don't want to hasten into another blunder here."

"Oh, Christ!" Lazlo swore.

McComb sat there on the floor of the cage, and listened. They were discussing his execution, and that of Nalin, as if they were not present. As if they were farm animals raised for butchery.

Camargue glared at Lazlo. "You brought this down on us. Now do not show us your anger because this must be done in the way of the Kris, the old tribunal. It appears the Fourth Crucifixion Nail has appeared in my tent, and I must follow the tradition closely, or suffer consequences."

Camargue referred to the Gypsy legend that it was a Gypsy who forged the nails for the crucifixion of Christ, but that only three of the four were used. When trouble came to any troupe, it was said that some Gypsies saw a sizzling hot nail appear in their tents, threatening them and forcing them to move on. That is why the Gypsies are nomads, the legend said.

126

"Tradition!" Lazlo hissed out. "Tradition will be the death of you, old man!"

"I'm sorry, Yuray, but I must go along with Antoine," Idranyi said quietly. "This is a serious matter that must be done in the right way."

Lazlo glared at him.

"We will have a Kris meeting tomorrow morning," Antoine announced. "The fate of this man, and the girl, will be decided at that time."

Idranyi nodded, and turned to Lazlo. "Before we retire, though, I have news that will be of interest to Yuray, and also the rest of us."

Camargue had started to leave, but now turned back to his son-in-law. Kitta frowned slightly and came over closer to her husband. Lazlo was somber-faced.

"It was when I was buying our flour and spices. I overheard another customer tell the storekeeper that Yuray's friend Emmett Skinner is definitely in the area now. He was seen south of here, on a lame horse."

Lazlo's face changed subtly, and the frustration went out of it. "You heard that?" he said softly.

Inside the cage, McComb sat there and listened and sighed heavily.

"The fellow who told it seemed to know what he was talking about," Idranyi said. "Skinner identified himself to this drifter, and he was asking about McComb." He glanced into the cage. "Seems he's got a kind of obsession about killing him."

McComb glared at him.

A little whimpering sound came from Nalin's

127

throat. She had been raped by Skinner, too, and knew he was even an uglier man than Yuray Lazlo. In the cage, McComb was having the same thoughts run through his head.

Kitta was laughing. "What an irony," she said. "Skinner is probably on his way to join us right now. And when he gets here, it won't matter what we decide about McComb."

Lazlo grinned. "Oh, Mule will be here, all right. And when he gets here, McComb will wish he was already dead and buried."

Idranyi returned the grin, but it was not as broad as Lazlo's. He did not like killing, particularly. It could produce consequences that were troublesome.

"None of this bodes well," Camargue muttered, as he turned again, and left.

"Come, Vaclav," Kitta said to her husband. "It is late, and we are keeping the boy awake."

Idranyi nodded. In the cage, McComb noticed that he wore a ring of keys on his belt, and figured one of them unlocked the door at the rear of his cage. "Get some sleep, Yuray," Idranyi said to Lazlo. "We will talk more of these two in the morning."

Lazlo nodded, and grabbed Nalin by the wrist and yanked her along to his wagon with him. He knew that Skinner would find them in a short time, and he liked that idea. He would then persuade Idranyi to leave the troupe and ride with him and Skinner, and leave Camargue to his Gypsy traditions. Nalin made some more sobbing sounds as he

128

dragged her away, with her trying to cast one last look at McComb. Idranyi left with Kitta, and suddenly McComb was alone at the cage again.

He was very weak after the exertion. But he found the bread that Nalin had brought to him, and he grabbed it from under the blanket and ate it hungrily, as an animal would. When he was finished, he leaned back against the end of the wagon and considered the situation. It was possible that Camargue would be persuaded to kill him tomorrow, even though he doubted that Camargue would allow Lazlo to kill Nalin. But just as importantly, McComb figured Skinner already knew about Camargue's presence in the area, would have deduced that Lazlo was still with the Gypsy family, and would come to join back up with Lazlo. McComb also did not doubt for a moment that Skinner intended to kill him if he got the chance. And if he knew Skinner, the killing would not be an easy one.

That meant that McComb had to escape from the Gypsies, and take Nalin with him. Preferably, on this very night. He glanced up at the sky, and saw that it was clouded over now. Off in the prairie somewhere, a coyote howled at the darkness.

With a modest increase in strength now from the bread, McComb crawled to the end of the cage with the door in it, and tried the door once again. It was locked from the outside, as he had concluded previously. He pushed hard against it, and it rattled some in place, but did not otherwise budge. He went to the wall of bars on his right, and reached his hand through the bars, and around to the edge of the back side of the wagon. He could feel the separation where the door met the body of the wagon, and then he felt a slide bolt. He managed to inch his fingers onto the bolt, and was able to slide it away from him, and out of its receiving end. With his left hand that was still inside the cage, he pushed again on the door and it would not move any more than before. He was getting out of breath with exertion now. He felt below the slide bolt, and found a padlock hanging on another lock.

He brought his arm back in, and swore under his breath. His shoulder hurt from the strain, and his forearm was scraped red from the wood of the wagon. He rested. Then he put his feet up against the door and kicked at it, hoping the release of the slide bolt would weaken the door enough to allow him to force it open. He kicked several times, and it held.

McComb was completely exhausted, and realized he could do nothing more that night. He reached outside once again, replaced the sliding bolt to its original, locked position, and fell heavily to the floor of the wagon, collapsing from fatigue.

When he woke, it was almost dawn.

In a short time, the camp was up, with Ranko out and kicking the fire up. Vali came over to the wagon while the others were preparing for a morning meal, and harassed McComb by throwing pebbles and clumps of hard dirt into the wagon. Then Kitta called him away, and the family gathered at the far side of camp, out of earshot, and the men had their palaver about McComb. McComb strained to hear, but could not. Finally it was over, and McComb saw Lazlo walk away from the others in a huff. A moment later, Antoine Camargue came over to McComb.

"I believe you are entitled to know your fate, Mc-Comb. You have been sentenced to death by the family."

McComb sat there, and a lead weight formed in his chest. He had hoped otherwise, because of the way Lazlo had reacted to the talk.

"We will not do it here, we are too close to the settlement," Camargue went on, as if discussing an act in their show. "We will move west, into the Great Basin. You will go with us, at least for today." He paused meaningfully. "Lazlo wanted to kill you now. He also wanted to dispose of the girl. That will not happen. I intend to set her loose in an appropriate place, so she will cause us no more trouble."

The weight in McComb's chest lightened some. He nodded. "Thanks," he said.

Camargue sighed. "I am sorry about this. But we must protect the family." A moment later he turned and left.

They moved out within the hour, with the canvas down again over the cage wagon, so McComb could not see where they were going. But he knew better than they did where they were. He could tell from the position of the sun outside the canvas, and the terrain they were passing over, under the wheels of the wagon.

He did not see Nalin all that day. The wagon train traveled west all through a very long day, and the men whipped the horses to get more speed from them. When they finally camped after dark, McComb figured they must be most of a hundred miles from Fort Bonneville. However, if his deductions were correct, they were in Shoshoni territory now.

The canvas was raised again on the camp side of the cage wagon, about an hour after the train arrived at its stopping place, and Camargue himself brought McComb a cup of hot broth. McComb took it from the older man without speaking. McComb looked around the new camp, and Nalin was nowhere in sight. He hoped they had not dropped her off in the middle of nowhere already.

"This will be your last meal," Camargue said to McComb, rather apologetically. McComb swallowed hard. "I would like for it to be a better one, but we are poor people."

McComb stared at him. "Where is Nalin?"

Camargue waved a hand. "She is all right. I have ordered that she be taken from Lazlo until we can leave her near a Shoshoni village."

"The Shoshoni don't like Apaches," McComb said.

Camargue smiled. His face looked wrinkled and old under the narrow-brimmed hat, and his shirt and pants appeared baggy and soiled. "I know. But they won't hurt her. I hope that thought will help you through the next hours. You

132

will die at dawn, McComb. I have a superstition about killing in the night."

McComb grunted. "Very civilized, Camargue."

Camargue did not respond. He left, and McComb drank the broth, and watched the Gypsies mill about the camp before they went to bed for the night. Then he spotted Nalin, across the campsite. She was chained to Camargue's wagon, on the ground, with a blanket under her. She looked as if she had been beaten by Lazlo. Her head hung down, and she looked very weak.

"Bastards," McComb growled in his throat.

He had to get out of this camp tonight, or he was a dead man. And there was no guarantee that Camargue could keep Lazlo from killing Nalin, especially since Camargue had forbidden Lazlo from bedding with her now.

McComb's only chance, he figured, was to try to force the cage door again tonight, when they were all asleep. But in the next couple of hours, at about midnight, an opportunity came to him that he had not anticipated.

The camp was absolutely still, and McComb could hear one of the older men snoring. Across the compound, Nalin hunched in a fetal position on the ground under the edge of Camargue's wagon, apparently asleep. Then Vaclav Idranyi stumbled out of his wagon.

He was sleepy-looking, and wore only his trousers. His dark hair was mussed, and his handsome face was slack-featured, his eyes hooded. He came to the middle of the camp, took a handful of himself out of his pants at the crotch, and began urinating on the guttering coals of the almost-dead campfire. Across the compound, Nalin stirred slightly.

McComb narrowed his dark blue eyes on Idranyi, and saw that the ring of keys still hung from Idranyi's belt. McComb held his breath for a moment, then pressed up against the cage bars.

"Hey. Idranyi."

Idranyi was just stuffing himself back into his trousers. He glanced sleepily toward McComb. McComb sat back down, away from the bars. "Can you spare a minute?" he said to Idranyi.

Idranyi sighed heavily, yawned, and walked over to the cage wagon. "Yeah? What is it, McComb?"

"You could have saved me, Idranyi," McComb said quietly.

Idranyi looked at him. "Why should I?"

McComb grunted. He lay back on an elbow, acting weaker than he was. He held the tin cup up. "Since I've got just a few hours, would you get me some water?"

Idranyi regarded McComb balefully. "You don't need any water, my friend. You won't have time to digest it."

McComb sighed. "Then at least take this cup so I won't lay on it all night." He held it up again, but inside the bars, so Idranyi had to reach for it.

"Oh, hell," Idranyi grumbled. He reached inside the cage for the cup, so that his entire forearm came into the cage.

McComb struck at the arm like a diamondback

134

rattler, and grabbed it in an iron grip. He yanked hard on the arm, and Idranyi came crashing against the bars, hitting the side of his face there. McComb grabbed him by the neck with his free hand.

Idranyi was stunned, and breathing shallowly, his dark eyes round in sudden fear. *"What—the hell!"*

McComb looked down at Idranyi's hip, and saw that the keys were unreachable, without letting go of Idranyi. He swore softly.

"Now you listen to me," he growled.

Idranyi nodded abruptly. Blood was running down the side of his head from under his hair.

"Take the keys off your belt."

Idranyi hesitated, then complied.

McComb measured the distance to the end of the cage with his eyes, and saw they were close. "Take the right key, and unlock the cage door. You can reach it from there."

"I can't do that," Idranyi gasped out. "Lazlo would kill me."

McComb was wearing out fast. He jammed Idranyi's face against the bars, and Idranyi cried out softly. "Do it," he said. "Or I'll break your goddamn neck right now."

Idranyi glanced at McComb's muscular arms, and believed him. He reached out and put his hand around the corner of the wagon, and after a moment he found the padlock. He shoved the small key into it, and McComb heard the lock turn.

"Is it open?" McComb asked him.

Idranyi nodded.

"It had better be," McComb said. "Now drop the keys, and take the padlock off."

"Don't—make me do this," Idranyi gasped.

McComb tightened his strangle hold on Idranyi's throat. "Take it off," McComb growled. "And if you got any ideas of yelling for help, I wouldn't if I was you."

Idranyi hesitated again, then dropped the keys to the ground, and reached and took the padlock off the hinged lock. He dropped it to the ground, too. Across the campsite, Nalin looked over toward them, and saw what was happening.

McComb nodded when he saw the lock hit the ground. "Thanks," he said in a hard, low voice. Then he twisted with all his strength on Idranyi's neck.

There was an audible snapping sound, and Idranyi's eyes bulged for a moment, and choking sounds came from his throat. Then he slid from McComb's grasp, and hit the ground. He was dead. McComb had severed his cervical spine.

McComb sat there gasping harshly, unable to move for a moment. Finally, he went to the end of the cage, reached around the corner of it as he had done before, and slid the slide bolt out of its housing. From inside then, he pushed on the cage door, and it swung open.

He just sat there looking at the opening for a long moment. Then he stumbled out of the wagon. When his feet hit the ground, he fell onto his side.

He lay there breathing hard. Across the compound, Nalin sat up and stared at him, unbelieving.

136

She made no sound, though.

McComb rose to his feet, and felt very dizzy and weak. He listened to see if anybody was awake, and was satisfied that none were. He stumbled across the compound to Nalin.

"McComb!" she whispered to him, when he arrived.

He put a hand to his lips, and knelt beside her. He had picked up the ring of keys and brought it with him, and now he examined the big lock on the chain that bound Nalin's right ankle. He tried a couple of keys into the lock, and they did not work.

"I think Lazlo still has the key to this lock," Nalin whispered softly.

"Goddamn it!" McComb swore angrily under his breath. He looked into her face, and found a bruise on it. He touched the place gently.

"Lazlo keeps the key in his pocket, and he wears a gun," she whispered to him. "There is no way you can get it away from him. Not in your condition, McComb."

McComb looked over to Lazlo's wagon. "I can't leave here without you," he said heavily. He felt very dizzy again. "I wish that bastard Idranyi had had his gun with him." He yanked hard at the chain where it was affixed to the wagon, but it held firm. "Son of a bitch!"

Nalin put her slight hand on his bearded face. "Listen to me. Camargue will not kill me. You must save yourself. You must leave now, without delay. Maybe you will have luck and they will not be able to find you out there, when

137

they go searching tomorrow morning. Then you will be able to go for help."

"I don't know, Nalin."

"Please. It is our only hope, McComb."

He sighed very heavily. He did not like to leave her with these crazies. But she was right, he had to admit it. If he did not leave immediately, his chances of getting away were reduced greatly. And he could not free Nalin, there was just no way.

"All right," he finally said. "But I'll be back, Nalin. I'll come back for you."

She reached up and touched her lips to his. "Be careful, my lover. I will await patiently for your return."

He looked into her lovely, dark eyes for a moment, then turned and crept away, out of the compound.

In just moments, he had left the encampment behind. Nobody followed him. He staggered onward, and put the camp out of sight. He looked around him in the night, and got his bearings. He recognized the hulking silhouette of a rugged butte in the distance. He turned and headed southwest.

He had a long night ahead of him.

Chapter Seven

All during that long, black night, McComb tried to hide his trail. If he made too obvious a track in a sandy area, he went back and rubbed it out with a swatch of brush, in the Apache way. Whenever he could travel over rock or hard ground, he did. Just before dawn, he had to lie down and rest for an hour, and he briefly fell asleep. He dreamed, and he was back at the Gypsy camp, and they had tied him to a wagon, and Lazlo was preparing to execute him with a shotgun.

When he awoke, the sun was already up, and it was a clear morning. He got up, and looked around. He was certain that if he continued southwest, he would soon be in Silver Wolf's territory. But he was also sure that it was a long way off, maybe as much as fifty miles.

The day turned hot by late morning, and McComb was becoming dehydrated. He had only the cut-off rawhides on his hips and thighs, and otherwise no protection. By noon he was weakened and burned from the sun, and he lay down under the sparse shade of a mesquite tree for rest. But he knew he must keep moving, or they might find him, and that would mean sudden death.

The afternoon was blast-furnace hot, more like summer than late spring. The sun was like a flatiron on McComb's neck and back. At one point he fell without knowing it, and woke up on the ground, sand in his mouth.

In midafternoon he almost stepped on a rattlesnake. It struck at him, and missed, and he grabbed at it behind the head, the way he had learned from the Indians. He broke its neck, found a sharp stone to skin it with, and ate part of it. He stuck some more of its meat in his waistband, and started off again, with more strength. An hour later he found a pear cactus, and cut the end of a branch with the same sharp stone, and let the water from it run into his mouth and throat.

Those two finds got him through the day. Every half hour or so he would look to the horizon behind him, to see if he could spot riders. But none came. When the sun set, he found shelter under a scraggly pine tree, and passed the night there.

He did not want to continue the next morning. He wanted to lie under the tree and rest forever there. But his life depended on his keeping moving. His, and maybe Nalin's.

The terrain became drier as he walked that second day. He found another clump of cactus, but there was little water in it. He looked for a yew tree to find a branch that he could fashion into a bow, but was not successful. Noon came again, and the heat was becoming unbearable, and he began staggering by midafternoon. In late afternoon, when it felt as if he were enclosed in a pig-iron smelter, he began hallucinating. He had traveled toward Silver Wolf's Shoshoni village, and now he kept seeing tipis and wickiups that were not really there, and men and women milling around him. But they were afraid of him for some reason, and would not offer him help. He cried out once for water, and could not understand when none was brought to him.

Less than an hour after the hallucinations began, McComb collapsed. He lay facedown on hard ground, lost to the real world. His flesh was burned and his lips were cracked dry, but he did not feel any of that now. Turkey buzzards circled and circled overhead against a hard cobalt sky, and then they began landing on the dry ground near him, investigating in their neck-craned, glassy-stare manner, their red and black heads bobbing as they moved awkwardly on foot. When they found out he was helpless, they would come in on him and begin picking him to pieces. Men had had their eyeballs popped and their skulls picked clean inside by birds like these.

But McComb was not aware of the danger. He had regressed back to that awful, bloody day at Goliad, when his mother and father had been lined up against a stockade fence with the others who had surrendered to Santa Anna, and been shot down in cold blood. He could see, in his fevered head now, the hot lead hitting the captives in their bodies, making them jump and jerk and yell, and he saw his father hit, and then his mother. Then a Mexican soldier was restraining him from running to them, and there was a struggle between them, and he was slugged by something hard and he hit the ground on his side. Then the Mexican was standing over him and swearing at him, and his sister was sobbing loudly in the background.

"McComb!"

He stirred on the hard ground, and realized he had been dreaming, and thought the voice was one from the resurrected past. He felt a soft slap on his cheek.

"McComb, look at me!" In Shoshoni.

McComb's eyelids fluttered open, and hot sunlight flooded in. But there was a large silhouette blocking out a lot of the sky. It was Iron Knife, Chief Silver Wolf's son. McComb wondered if he were still hallucinating.

"Ah," Iron Knife said, when McComb focused on him. "What has happened to you, old friend?"

McComb reached out and touched Iron Knife's arm, and convinced himself the Indian was real. Behind Iron Knife stood two other warriors of the Shoshoni tribe, holding the reins of their mounts.

"I—" McComb could not form words. He grated out, over a swollen tongue, *"Help—me."*

Iron Knife nodded, then turned to the other Shoshonis. "Put him on a horse. We will take him back to the village."

A few minutes later, McComb was on his way to safety.

Back at the Gypsy encampment, Lazlo and Antoine Camargue had just returned from a long, frus-

142

trating two-day search for McComb. They rode into camp just before sunset, tired and dusty, and Yuray Lazlo was very sullen as he dismounted from his mustang stallion and picketed it to a wagon. Camargue looked ten years older. The boy Vali came and took his mount, and Camargue went and sat heavily on a camp stool beside a guttering fire. His brother Ranko and Madame Camargue stood nearby, and Kitta leaned against a wagon just a short distance away.

"You did not find him?" Ranko said to Camargue.

Camargue shook his head slowly. "The man travels like a ghost. The north wind makes more of a mark over its course. It is as if he just disappeared into the earth."

Kitta hit her small fist into the painted wood of the wagon, and swore under her breath. She had wanted to kill Nalin, when they found Idranyi dead at the cage on the previous morning. Instead, she went to the chained Indian girl and beat her mercilessly with a stick, until Ranko pulled her away. Nalin was still chained to the wagon, across the camp, bruised and weak from the beating and hunger. They had stopped feeding her, during Camargue's absence. Kitta's long hair hung onto her face now, and she pushed it back with her hand. Her pretty eyes were blazing with renewed anger.

"He killed my husband," she murmured harshly. "We cannot just let him go out there."

Madame had lost only a son-in-law, so was more stoic. "You play with fire, you get burned."

Lazlo and Kitta hurled acid looks at her. Camargue looked up at them. "He is gone. We cannot spend any more time looking for him. We were going west, anyway. We will leave this place tomorrow morning, and continue our trek to California. McComb cannot cause us trouble there."

Lazlo shook his head slowly. "If you had listened to me, old man, we wouldn't be having this conversation now. I told you to kill him. I knew he was trouble, as soon as I knew who he was. You should have done what I told you."

He had doffed a dark hat, and his curly black hair was now gray with dust. The hooded eyes looked mean, and the full mouth under the hooked nose was turned down at the corners. His brawny figure leaned against a nearby wagon not far from Kitta.

The elderly Ranko came and sat on a second camp stool near his brother. His white hair was uncombed, and his face looked a hundred years old this evening. "Yuray, you may not speak to our *Rom Baro* in this manner. It is a violation of our Marime Code, and a discourtesy in the family."

Lazlo gave the old fellow a brittle look. "To hell with the goddamn Marime Code," he said clearly and forcefully.

They all looked at him with sober faces. Camargue grunted. "You have never been a good Gypsy, Yuray. You have spent too much time with the *gajes*. You are not one of us now."

Lazlo knew that Camargue was right. He felt more comfortable with men like Emmett Skinner than he did with people like Camargue.

"Maybe not," he said sourly. "But you need me, Camargue. You think small. If we go to California

144

and finally find some wealth there, you will owe it to me. What capital you possess now, you owe to me."

Kitta regarded Lazlo soberly. She had never liked him, and could not understand why Idranyi had. She had heard Lazlo tell Idranyi once about a blond woman Lazlo had kidnapped from a ranch. He kept her in a tarpaulin for weeks, raping her at will, and then cut her tongue out when he released her, so she could not tell the law about him. Kitta figured her husband would still be alive if it were not for Lazlo.

"And Vaclav's death we owe to you," she said bitterly.

Lazlo regarded Kitta somberly. Now that Idranyi was gone, he would find a time and place that was right for tasting of Kitta's obviously delicious fruits. "Horse manure," he said.

"You brought the mountain man to us, Yuray," Camargue said to him. "Vaclav would not have done so, on his own."

Madame Camargue came between them, facing Camargue. "Enough of this bickering. What is done is done, Antoine." She was a very practical woman, and knew Lazlo's value to them. "Now we must forget the mountain man, and mourn our loss."

Over at the edge of camp, Vali was playing with a stick and ball. He had not shed a tear over his father, nor given any thought to his death, and Madame sadly realized that Kitta would have to raise a soulless youth who could become a worse man than Lazlo. She glanced out past the barrel-top and canvas-covered wagons with their gaily painted sides, to the hump of earth beyond that marked Idranyi's shallow grave, and felt a foreboding about the family that she had never had before. Madame believed in her power to look into the future, and honestly believed that she was giving the paying customers their money's worth when she told their fortunes in her crystal ball. She had looked into it that morning, all by herself, and had seen things that disturbed her greatly. A dark cloud hanging over their encampment, and a feeling of violence and terror. She had told no one.

"Tomorrow early," Camargue said heavily, "we will put some more distance between us and Fort Bonneville. We will head south for a couple of days, and then gradually turn our wagons west. There are some watering holes just to the west of —"

Camargue paused, and listened. They all heard the sound, too, and it was the sound of horse's hooves. Lazlo went to his mount and grabbed an old Plains rifle off its irons, and moved to the edge of camp toward which the rider was coming. The sun was almost down, and visibility was not as good as it had been just an hour earlier. They all squinted toward the oncoming rider, as he came at them beyond a cottonwood tree. Then he emerged into view, just outside the quadrangle of their wagons.

"Well, I'll be damned," Lazlo said under his breath.

Kitta recognized him next. "It's Emmett Skinner," she said in a sober voice.

Camargue rose from the stool, and stared toward the rider. He had always feared Skinner somewhat, even though Lazlo had ridden with him, and even Idranyi had accepted the man. As bad an influence on others as Lazlo could be, Camargue sensed that

Skinner was by far the worst of the two. Madame and Ranko looked toward Skinner blank-faced, and Vali came and stood beside his mother.

Out at the perimeter of the camp, Skinner sat his mount heavily, and gazed at the Gypsy camp before him. It had been a few days' hard riding to catch them, and he had had to track them from their last encampment near Fort Bonneville over difficult terrain. But now he had found them. Them, and Yuray Lazlo.

Skinner rode on into camp on his stolen Arabian mare, and Lazlo met him just inside the wagons.

"Well, I'll be damned!" Lazlo said again, more forcefully. There was no real affection between him and Skinner, because neither was capable of it. But they both had done very well in each other's company, and each looked at the other man as the other half of a very profitable partnership.

"Lazlo," Skinner said without smiling.

"Son of a bitch," Lazlo said. "We heard you were out, Mule. I thought you might try to find us."

Camargue came over, too. Skinner looked even bigger and more dangerous than he remembered him. "Welcome back, Skinner," he said courteously. He did not like Skinner, but he knew enough about men to treat Skinner cordially.

"Camargue," Skinner said. He hefted his bulk off the mare, and picketed the animal to the nearest wagon. "It's been a long ride. You got any coffee made?"

"Hell, yes," Lazlo answered for Camargue. "Come on over to the fire and shake the kinks out, Mule."

Skinner did not shake anybody's hand, or even greet them in the ordinary way. He nodded to Madame when he passed her, and then gave Kitta and Ranko a quick look. Kitta eyed him warily. She did not need another visit by Skinner, on top of everything else. Vali came and stood before Skinner, and spoke loudly to him.

"Hey, it's Skinner! You bring any stuff from the prison with you?"

Skinner eyed him with disdain. "Get out of the way, kid."

Vali stepped sidewise just in time to keep from getting bowled over as Skinner went and stood by the fire. Lazlo handed Skinner a cup of hot coffee, and Skinner swigged half of it as if it were lemonade. Most men would have yelled as it burned their mouths.

"Tell us about it, Mule," Lazlo said, grinning. His entire demeanor had changed. His face was animated with excitement. "How did you get out?"

Skinner enjoyed the deference paid him by Lazlo, that was one of the things that had kept them together, before. Lazlo was a tough guy, but he was no Skinner. Skinner was bigger, harder, more ruthless, and more dangerous. Lazlo knew that, and respected it.

"It was easy," Skinner said in his grating voice. "I just had to kill a couple of people." He looked over at Camargue, to see his reaction to that statement. Skinner loved to bully others with his menacing manner.

"I heard you were out awhile ago," Lazlo repeated himself. "How was it at Devil's Hole?"

148

Skinner grinned. "Like a Sunday picnic on the Ohio River," he said, swigging more of the coffee.

"Is the law on your trail?" Camargue asked him, seating himself again on the stool.

Skinner dropped a hard look on him. "The law ain't got no idea where I am, old man. Don't worry your head with it."

Ranko sat on his stool, eyeing Skinner darkly. This one would be harder to handle than Lazlo, he knew. He had seen enough of him on a previous occasion to know that Skinner took orders from nobody, and had no respect for the Rom. Madame stood near the fire, pulling a dark shawl around her shoulders. The last time Skinner came, there was the flash of gold around the camp. Madame liked the flash of gold. But she remembered the crystal ball vision, and wondered if Skinner were connected with it.

"Will you be staying with us for a while?" she asked Skinner.

Skinner looked over at her. "Not long, Madame. Not long."

"I'm going to go get some firewood," Kitta said, speaking to Madame. She turned and left without saying a word to Skinner. He grinned slightly as he watched her walk away.

"Is something eating her?" he said.

Lazlo sighed briefly. "We just lost Vack."

Skinner went and sat on a third camp stool, still holding the coffee cup. "Oh?"

"That's his grave over there," Lazlo said.

Skinner looked past the camp in the fading light, to the mound of earth out there in the encroaching darkness.

"How the hell did that happen?"

Camargue replied before Lazlo could. "A mountain man. A mountain man killed him."

Skinner grunted. "Tough luck. A mountain man put me in that stink hole for all that time." He turned to Lazlo. "That's why I come here. To get you to ride out with me to put that son of a bitch under ground."

Lazlo looked at the ground for a moment. "It was McComb that killed Idranyi, Mule."

Skinner's face changed as they all looked at him. "What?" he said in a guttural, ugly tone. "What did you say?"

Lazlo stepped back a half step unconsciously, not wanting to be too near Skinner's anger. "We had him here. Found him on the trail, wounded. Put him in the bear cage and made him part of the show. We didn't know it was McComb. Remember, I hadn't ever seen him."

Skinner rose and looked into Lazlo's face. "You had him here?" he said incredulously.

"We overheard him and the Indian girl talking, and then we knew." Lazlo pointed toward Nalin, across the compound, and Skinner looked over at her. He walked over there, and Nalin looked up at him warily. She had seen him ride in, and knew immediately who he was. This was a bad thing for her, Skinner's arrival. She wished McComb would hurry back with help.

"The goddamn Apache," Skinner muttered.

"It all happened a couple of days ago," Lazlo said. "He got Vack over to the cage, and killed him, and escaped. We rode out after him, but he just disappeared out there."

Skinner turned back to Lazlo. "You had the son of a bitch here," he said darkly. "And you let him escape."

Lazlo was afraid to respond to that. Skinner walked over to where the dray horses were picketed, and stood turned away from the others for a long moment. Then he hauled off and savagely kicked the nearest horse in the ribs.

The horse whinnied excitedly, and reared and almost broke its tether. A big cooking pan sat on a log at the edge of camp there, with some stew in it, ready to put on the fire. Skinner grabbed the pan and hurled it and its contents against a nearby tree. All the horses were now rearing and plunging. Skinner picked up a pile of pans and utensils, and hurled them, clattering, against the nearest wagon. Kitta came from another wagon, wide-eyed, wondering what had happened. Madame Camargue retreated to the far side of camp from Skinner, and Ranko got off his stool and huddled against a nearby wagon. Vali ran to his mother. Camargue and Lazlo just watched Skinner.

Skinner was breathing shallowly, getting himself under control. He finally turned back to Lazlo.

"You goddamn fool!" he grated out.

Lazlo averted his gaze, not wanting to look into those psychotic eyes. "I wanted to kill him, when we found out who he was. But they wouldn't." He gestured toward Camargue.

Skinner came over to him. *"They didn't know what he was! It was up to you!"*

Lazlo hung his head like a child. You did not argue with Skinner. It was bad for your health.

151

"If McComb hadn't killed that idiot Idranyi, I would have!" Skinner went on, less loudly.

Lazlo shot a private look at Camargue, and Camargue was sober-faced. Kitta turned abruptly, and disappeared again. Madame was expressionless.

"I'm sorry, Mule," Lazlo offered. "You're right, I should have shot the bastard. I should have killed him when I could."

Skinner eyed him fiercely, but Lazlo's admission of guilt seemed to appease him. "Son of a bitch," he said bitterly. "I been tracking that half man ever since I got loose."

"God knows where he is now," Lazlo said, still not understanding. "Antoine here wants to move on west and south tomorrow, and forget about McComb. You going with us?"

Skinner looked at Lazlo as if he had suddenly gone crazy. "Forget about McComb? What the hell has happened to you, Lazlo? You lost some marbles since I seen you? We ain't forgetting McComb. To hell with moving out of here. Let them do what they feel like, later." He jerked a thumb toward Camargue. "You and me are going after that goddamn trapper. We're going to find him, and we're going to make him die slow. Then we're going to make us some real money. I got some ideas that will make us rich, by Jesus."

Lazlo's face brightened again. With Skinner back, he did not need the family anymore. He was ready to go out and raise some hell again. Vack had been all right, but he had never had the aggressiveness to ever hit it big. And he had always had Camargue looking over his shoulder, telling him what he should or should not do. Even though Lazlo was a Gypsy himself, he was feeling less and less loyalty to the family, or the tribe. He did not want the Marime Code or Romania anymore, he had had enough of Camargue's small thinking. Skinner was more his type.

"That sounds just fine to me, Mule," he responded to Skinner. He turned to Camargue. "Well, Antoine. Do you want to stay put here until we locate that mountain man? If not, I guess this is where we split company."

Madame and Ranko turned to hear Camargue's reply.

"I will give this some thought," he said seriously. He tried a weak smile, hoping to keep the goodwill of this outsider who had already wrought physical and emotional havoc in their midst. "You will eat with us, Skinner, and get a good night's sleep here. Then we will discuss this McComb tomorrow morning, when we are all fresh. Is that acceptable?"

Ranko frowned slightly toward him. Camargue would never have solicited Lazlo's agreement.

"Hell, I wouldn't have started out for him tonight, anyway," Skinner said with absolutely no deference. "We can talk about it in the morning."

Lazlo grunted his approval. "Now, the other problem is that Apache woman." He recalled that Camargue was in favor of releasing Nalin, but Lazlo did not like that idea. He had abused her too badly. "She's no good to me anymore, and no good to the family."

Nalin, over at the wagon where she was chained, heard her name mentioned, and looked toward Lazlo, new fear in her face.

"Problem?" Skinner said in the ugly voice. "Why, that ain't no problem, Lazlo."

Skinner walked over to Nalin, drew the Derringer Navy .54 from its holster, aimed it casually at Nalin's head, and squeezed the trigger.

Nalin did not have time to realize the significance of this turn of events. Suddenly the gun exploded loudly in the compound, and the lights went out for her forever. As Camargue and Madame looked on in shock, Nalin's head whiplashed as if she had been hit with a club, and then she slid to one side, motionless. Behind her on the painted side of the wagon was a mess of bone and blood.

Skinner reholstered the gun almost distractedly. "Now let's see what you got to eat around here," he said.

Chapter Eight

McComb's eyelids fluttered open on a crisp, pristine morning. The awful heat of the previous day was gone, and the air smelled good. There was the redolent aroma of cooking food, and of a wood fire. He lay on a pallet in a large tipi made of animal skins, and it was all familiar to him. He had slept in this very structure before, when visiting Silver Wolf for trading.

Outside the skin tent, McComb could hear voices in Shoshoni, and the sounds of children playing. He raised himself up onto an elbow in the dim morning light, and felt weak. He remembered them giving him food and water on his arrival the evening before, and he recalled Iron Knife's face looking into his own with great concern. He had been lucky. He had hoped he was heading toward the village of Silver Wolf, and that they might find him out there if he succumbed to the elements, and they had.

The flap of the tipi opened, and Silver Wolf came in.

"Ah, our visitor awakes." He smiled and sat down on a ground cover beside McComb. He was a strong-looking fellow in his fifties, with gray hair and a leathery face. He had vowed to try to live in harmony with the white man, and accept their intrusions into his land. But he considered himself the sole proprietor of that land, and that the white man was here through his sufferance. It had not even occurred to him that the white man might one day be dictating terms to him in his own homeland. The white men he had met so far were mostly like McComb, and Silver Wolf liked McComb. He and his son had hunted with McComb, and gone trapping with him, and Iron Knife had slept in McComb's bed, at his cabin.

"Good morning, Silver Wolf," McComb replied in good Shoshoni. "It appears I owe my life to you, and to Iron Knife."

"You owe it to the Great Spirit, who guided you to our village," Silver Wolf said with a smile. "You knew you would be found in this territory, and by friends."

"Well. I want to thank you for everything you've done," McComb said.

"You did the same for Iron Knife, when the cougar attacked him," Silver Wolf reminded him. "Your expression of gratitude is unnecessary and inappropriate."

McComb shook his head. Few men had a feeling for personal relationships like Silver Wolf. "All right, Silver Wolf. But you will excuse me, I'm sure, if I have a special feeling of friendship for you and your son this morning."

Silver Wolf nodded. He was dressed plainly at the moment, with rawhide trousers and shirt, and a couple of eagle feathers in his hair. "That is appropriate," he said. "You were in ill form when you came to us, Long Hunter. You were without proper clothing, and you had been mistreated, it seemed. I had our medicine man treat you while you slept."

McComb remembered now. He awakened a couple of times with a weird mask hanging over his head, worn by a wiry, bronze figure, and a bag of bones was being shook over him, and there was a stench of something burning in the air.

"Well, it must have helped," McComb said. "I feel much better this morning."

"Your body still needs healing water," Silver Wolf told him. He frowned slightly. "Who did this thing to you, my son?"

McComb sighed heavily. "Gypsies," he replied.

"Ah," Silver Wolf said in his throat, and he made a sour face. "It is to be expected from them. Some trade with them, but we will not. They are a strange tribe, more like us than the white tribe, and less so. They do not possess personal integrity." He offered McComb a trade cigar.

McComb looked past him. "I guess there are some good ones. But these have fallen in with some bad people. They have my Apache woman." He accepted the cigar, and nodded.

"Ah. Yes." The cigar was lighted, and McComb sucked on it.

"I must go back and get her," McComb said.

"There is a Gypsy party north of here one day's ride. My braves have seen them."

"That's them," McComb told him. "That's Camargue's group."

"And they have misused your woman?" Silver Wolf said.

McComb hesitated, remembering. "Yes."

"I can give you some warriors to return there with you," Silver Wolf said.

McComb shook his head. "No, there would be bloodshed by Shoshonis, and the white men at Fort Bonneville would misunderstand. I will not put you in that position."

"We do not concern ourselves with misunderstandings, when a friend may be helped."

McComb smiled. "I know. But this is my problem, Silver Wolf. I must go for Nalin alone. I need a mount, and a gun."

"They are yours, Long Hunter," Silver Wolf told him.

"You may bring the woman here for care, if she needs it," the chieftain added. "But she may not spend the night in our village, McComb. She is Apache."

McComb smiled inside, where it did not show. He was well aware that Nalin would not have been treated much better here, with the Shoshonis, than she had been at the hands of the Gypsies. Unless it were known that she was McComb's woman.

"I understand, Silver Wolf," McComb said.

"Now, we will get you some good Shoshoni food," Silver Wolf told him. "You must be strong, for the undertaking you are to start out upon."

McComb nodded. He sat up and the light skin blanket dropped off him, and he was still bare to the waist. He looked very primitive, with the hairy chest and the thick beard, even more so than Silver Wolf.

"Your kindness warms me, old friend," McComb said.

The tipi flap opened again, and Iron Knife came in. McComb smiled at him as the younger man came and sat beside his father. "You are looking well, McComb."

"If you had not found me, I would be vulture bait by now," McComb said. He puffed on the cigar. It was a very stale one.

Iron Knife's face went somber, and his father and McComb regarded him curiously. Ordinarily, if all present were Indians, Iron Knife would have had to exchange many formalities and maybe even smoke a pipe, before he got on with any serious discussions. But he knew that McComb did not expect that.

"I have news for you, my friend."

McComb frowned slightly. "Yes?"

"I returned alone to find the Gypsies after I brought you here. You were mumbling about them in your sleep, and I knew where they were located."

Silver Wolf was surprised. He had known that his son was gone through the night, but had not known about this. "You went without my counsel, my son."

Iron Knife lowered his eyes. "Yes, Father. There was no time for a formal palaver. Excuse me."

Silver Wolf nodded. "Go on."

"I went to the Gypsy camp, unseen. I was hidden in a clump of granjeno, and they never knew I was there. I was only fifty yards from their camp."

McComb did not like the long look on Iron Knife's face. He frowned, and waited.

"It was not to spy for you, McComb," he said, now going into English from his own language. "We always try to keep our eyes on all those who encroach into our ancient land. To see what they intend."

"Yes, of course," McComb said.

"The man you put in jail was there," Iron Knife went on.

McComb's gut tightened up. "Shit."

"He appeared very angry," Iron Knife said.

McComb nodded. "That would be because he missed finding me there. He wants to kill me."

Iron Knife sighed heavily. "Your woman was there, McComb."

McComb held his gaze. "Yes. I know."

"The man called Skinner, the one you put in jail. He shot your woman."

McComb felt a lead weight grow inside him. "Oh, my God."

"She is dead, McComb," Iron Knife concluded.

McComb sat there, numb. He had told her he would be back, that he would come for her. He had promised her.

"Oh, my God," he repeated. He put the cigar out.

Iron Knife turned to his father and repeated it all in Shoshoni, because Silver Wolf did not understand much English. Silver Wolf's face was very somber. He reached over and touched McComb's shoulder. "You have our deepest sympathy, Long Hunter."

McComb nodded, putting a hand over his eyes and closing them tightly. "I should never have left her. Goddamn it, I should never have left her."

Iron Knife shook his head slowly. "I saw her, she

was chained to a wagon. I suspect she was that way when you made your escape."

McComb sat there, finally nodded almost imperceptibly.

"You did it the only way you could have," Iron Knife said. "You cannot blame yourself for another man's evil acts."

McComb opened his eyes and stared across the small space of the tipi interior. Sunlight slanted in past the entrance and fell in a golden bar across the ground covers around them. But he could find nothing golden about the morning. He rose awkwardly, his breathing coming more shallowly. The two Indians also stood.

"Get me some clothes," he said in a low monotone. "I'm — going after that son of a bitch. And this time, I'm not turning him over to the law."

"Let me go with you, Long Hunter," Iron Knife said.

McComb shook his shaggy head. "No, friend. This is personal. I have to do it myself."

Iron Knife nodded. "Let it be so," he said.

It took most of the rest of that morning to get McComb ready to leave. He was outfitted with shirt, pants, and moccasins, and given an Indian pony and a rusty-looking old one-shot pistol that he doubted he could really kill anybody with. Then, at just after the noon meal they gave him, McComb rode off for Fort Bridger.

That was not a direct route back to the Gypsy wagon encampment, but McComb figured the detour would be worthwhile. He rode all that day on the Indian pony, bareback, and without a hat. He rode around the south end of the Great Salt Lake all through the end of that day, and most of the next one. On the third day he arrived at the settlement.

He was only there overnight. He bought a buckskin outfit that fit him better, and a dark Stetson hat, at the store where they knew him and where he had credit. Then he heard that his pinto stallion and its gear had been sold recently to a local hostler, and McComb walked over to the livery the next morning.

It was a large clapboard building with the odor of manure and hay, and McComb liked the smells. Even before he spotted the hostler, he saw his pinto, standing in a stall, with its saddle and gear hanging on a hook nearby. On a shelf across the big room were McComb's saddle scabbards with the long guns still in them, and even the Patterson-Colt revolver was there, in its holster. McComb knew that the Gypsies had taken his stuff to Fort Bonneville to sell it, but the buyer must have brought it all here to re-sell. Traders often bought at one settlement and sold at another, where the market might be better for that particular item.

"Can I help you, mister?"

McComb turned to see the aging hostler standing behind him.

"Well, I'll be a horny toad!" the man said when he saw McComb's face. "If it ain't McComb!"

McComb nodded to him. He was a middle-aged fellow with balding, graying hair and wire-rimmed spectacles. His name was Kravitz "How are you making out, Kravitz?"

162

"Just dandy, McComb. I see you looking at that stallion there. Looks a lot like the one you ride, don't he?"

"It's the same animal," McComb said.

The hostler frowned. "Well, I'll be damned."

"It was stolen from me. Along with all this other gear here. By Gypsies."

"Well, I'll be damned," Kravitz said.

McComb let a deep breath out. "Look, Kravitz. I think you know that title to stolen property don't go to any buyer of it. The stuff is still mine. But when I get back past here, I'll drop off a few beavers for you, to make up your loss."

Kravitz sighed. Then he nodded. "I won't deprive any man of his stolen property. You take it all away, McComb. And you don't owe me nothing."

"You took a loss," McComb said. "I'll be back by here later to make it up to you some."

"Well. Thanks, McComb."

Within an hour, McComb was riding out of Fort Bridger on his own pinto, with his own guns on the mount's flanks, and the revolver strapped to his hip and thigh.

It was a three-day ride to where he last saw the Gypsy camp.

With a burning hatred now in his chest, that was where he was headed.

In Camargue's camp, Emmett Skinner was a surly, fearsome addition to the small group.

He had taken Lazlo out into the dry basin country for several days in a row, trying to pick up McComb's trail, but had been unsuccessful. Every day they rode back into camp, dusty and tired, Skinner had grown more and more difficult to be around.

Even Lazlo was glad to get away from him, at the end of those days. He had never seen Skinner in such a foul mood.

At just about the same time that McComb was leaving Fort Bridger to locate the Gypsies again, Camargue called a meeting that same morning, to discuss the future of the group. Skinner was not interested in any meeting, but Camargue brought the others to him, over at the edge of the campsite, and they all gathered around to hear what Camargue had to say. All but Kitta and her son, that is. Kitta wanted nothing to do with Skinner, since he had killed Nalin in cold blood. She had urged Camargue, privately, to ask Skinner and Lazlo both to leave.

"It is clear," Camargue was saying to the others, when they had gathered about, "that we are not going to find McComb now. He is either dead, or has been rescued."

"He ain't dead," Skinner said, leaning arrogantly against a nearby wagon.

They all looked at him for a moment. Camargue, his wife, Ranko, Lazlo. Lazlo was secretly fed up with looking for McComb, but did not want to risk Skinner's ire by making an issue of it.

Camargue sighed heavily. "Perhaps not, Skinner. But you must admit that it is becoming clear that he is no longer in the vicinity of this camp."

Skinner grunted. He had already come to the same conclusion. But he figured he knew McComb better than these people. "That's right," he said in his grating voice. "But he'll be back, Camargue."

Camargue held his sober gaze.

"He'll come for his Indian," Skinner said.

Lazlo coughed out a short laugh. "That won't do him any good," he said.

Camargue gave him a hard look, and let his gaze drift over to the second mound of dirt, just outside of camp, where Nalin's body was buried.

"He'll come faster, if he finds out I killed her," Skinner went on. His thick-set torso seemed to meet his head without the intervention of a neck, and Camargue thought his meat-crowded eyes reminded him of those of a hog they had once owned. He wore the dungaree outfit he had stolen from the people he had killed since his escape from prison, and an old felt hat on his head. "That's why I done it."

"We met a drummer on the trail out there," Lazlo said. "He was headed south, so we told him about Nalin. Scared the hell out of him. Maybe he'll take the word to McComb, wherever he is."

Camargue looked from Skinner to Lazlo. Even though Lazlo was one of them, he was a little like the crazy Skinner. Kitta was right, the family would be better with them both gone. Skinner could bring them money, but he could also bring the law down on them, or the wrath of others. And he was a continuing personal threat to every member of the family, because of his ruthlessness.

"Mule wants to stay put right here for a while, figuring McComb will be here sooner or later, if he thinks the Apache is still here. Or if he finds out she's dead, he'll come for Skinner," Lazlo told Camargue.

Ranko, sitting beside the campfire, looked at

Lazlo. "I have no interest in this McComb. The family has no further interest in him. It is in the family's best interests to move on to California. Particularly since McComb's escape. He may bring the law down on us now. We must move on, and let Mister Skinner do as he wishes."

Camargue looked quickly toward Skinner, to see his reaction. Skinner regarded Ranko balefully. "I was surprised to see you still alive, old man. I thought the family would just have set you out for the coyotes to tear at." He laughed loudly then, in a guttural way that sent a little shiver down Madame Camargue's back.

"We take care of our own," she said quietly to Skinner.

He stopped laughing, and gave her a diamond-hard look that made her hold her breath for a moment.

"Don't get the notion I need you people to handle McComb," Skinner finally said to Camargue, not responding to Madame. "I need you for bait. McComb might not find me, if you ain't here. And I want him to find me."

A heavy silence hung over the encampment for a long moment.

"When and if McComb comes, it will not be safe for our women, and the boy," Camargue said after a time. "What I suggest, as a compromise, is that we send them away, with my brother here. They may take two wagons and most of the provisions, and start west. There are only Shoshonis in that direction, and most of them are friendly. I will remain here with you, Skinner, and Yuray. After your confrontation with McComb, I will rejoin the others at the earliest opportunity. I can shoot a gun. I will help you in any way you want, with McComb."

Lazlo nodded, and looked over at Skinner. "That sounds all right, doesn't it, Mule? Hell, we don't need the women, anyway."

Skinner came and squatted by the fire, and his bulk was intimidating there. He finally looked up at Camargue. "Okay, Camargue. Get rid of the others. But I want two of the wagons here. To attract McComb."

Camargue nodded. "It is agreed."

Madame rose from a seated position on a stool. "I will go advise Kitta," she said.

Ranko got up, too. "The family splits. It is a bad omen." Then he too turned and went to a wagon and disappeared there.

Skinner shook his head. "Why do you keep that old idiot around, for God's sake? He'd be better off with a bullet in his head."

Camargue narrowed his dark eyes on Skinner, but said nothing. Lazlo intervened quickly. "He's harmless, Mule. Nobody pays him any mind."

"I will go help the others pack up," Camargue said, rising. "The sooner they are gone, the better."

"Don't strain your back, Camargue," Skinner called after him, grinning and shaking his head. He turned to Lazlo then, when they were alone. "What the hell do you keep coming back to these people for?"

Lazlo shrugged. "I needed them, for a while. I had a place to rest my head. You were behind bars, and you know I'm no good alone, Mule."

167

"You ain't much good, anyway," Skinner said, not smiling.

Lazlo averted his eyes from that hard stare.

"You don't know why I got to kill that son of a bitch McComb, do you, Lazlo?"

Lazlo shrugged. "He put you in that stink hole."

"You know what it's like to sit in a place like that for all them months, scratching at lice and bedbugs, having roaches crawl over your goddamn face in your sleep? Eating that shit they call food, and drinking putrid water? Looking at four gray walls twenty-four hours of the day, every day, and not knowing if you'll ever get out? You got any idea, Lazlo?"

Lazlo looked into those hard, little eyes. "I guess not."

"I thought of that wild man every day and every night. Especially at night. I killed him in a hundred different ways, Lazlo. Until I boiled it down to a few choice ones. I still got them ways stored up in my head." He glanced over at Lazlo. "When he comes, don't make the mistake of killing him yourself, Lazlo."

Lazlo swallowed back a small fear. "Okay, Mule."

"You can cripple him if you have to, to save yourself. But don't kill him, by Jesus. His death is going to be a goddamn Blackfeet masterpiece. They know best how to make it last. I learned a few ways from them."

"I'll remember, Mule."

An hour later, two of the wagons rolled away, with Kitta, her son, Madame, and Ranko in them.

Camargue looked after them until they were out of sight.

Now we wait, he thought.

Wait for a bloody vengeance to act itself out in the rocky, dry country of the Great Basin.

Then maybe he would be rid of the madman.

Chapter Nine

McComb was following the Great Salt Lake around its northern end now.

It was his second day out from Fort Bridger. He was not eating well, or sleeping well. The lead weight in his gut would not go away. Even though he had not formally married Nalin, she had been the only woman he had ever cared for. He could still see her face on that dark night that he left her there, with the love in it, and the trust in him. A trust that assured her that when he said he would come back to save her, she could count on his promise. There had been no doubt in that lovely face. Fear, yes, but not doubt.

She had counted on McComb to come through for her.

He had let her down.

He thought it would have been easier for him to have learned they had already killed her, when he first arrived in the Gypsy camp. To get her back, and then lose her in this way, was almost intolerable to him.

The only thing that kept him going, kept him moving out on the trail now, was his deep, animal hatred for Skinner. At Devil's Hole, they had allowed a monster to escape, after McComb had put him there. Then McComb himself had allowed him to come back and kill the woman they had taken from him.

It all created such an anger inside him, such a roaring fire in his head, that he thought at first it might overwhelm him. But now it had congealed into a deadly resolve.

Skinner had murdered Nalin, McComb was certain, to get to him. To make McComb come at him like a crazy man, let down his defenses, and allow Skinner to kill him.

Well, McComb thought, it would be decided soon who would do the killing, and who would end up buzzard food on the dusty plain.

The second day was half gone when McComb came upon the Indian just off the trail.

McComb had had a midday meal over a low fire about an hour before, and the day had turned cool and overcast since then. He was riding along hunched in his saddle, thinking how different the weather was from the heat when he had collapsed in the sun and been found by Iron Knife. He passed some granjeno, growing off to the side of the trail on a low hill, when he saw the moccasined feet protruding from the scrub brush.

McComb reined in the stallion and looked around, wondering if there was anyone else about. There did not appear to be. He dismounted and led the pinto over to the bushes. Lying there in an awkward sprawl was a Shoshoni brave.

McComb looked around a second time. Then he picketed the horse to one of the bushes and knelt over the fallen man.

He was young, just a kid really. He had blood on his face, his chest, and his left arm. His rawhide shirt had been torn away, and deep wounds were revealed across his chest. Shallower ones showed in the blood on his face. His eyes were open, and he saw McComb bend over him.

"A—cougar," the young man said in Shoshoni.

McComb nodded, and looked up into the rocks above him. He looked back down then into the Shoshoni's face. It looked ashen from shock. "You are of Silver Wolf's tribe," McComb said to him.

The fellow nodded. "You are—Long Hunter."

"When did this happen?" McComb asked.

"Very recently. You scared the animal off. It was—very large. It was preparing—to devour me."

McComb nodded, and inspected the young man's wounds. They looked awful, especially the ones across the chest. They were down to bone, and a lot of flesh had been torn out.

"Just a moment," McComb told him.

McComb went to his saddlebags, and got some gauze he always kept there for first aid, and a small bottle of whiskey. He came back and poured the whiskey on the fellow's wounds, and then bandaged his chest. He cleaned the face wounds, and the shallow ones on his arm. But he feared the Shoshoni was going into shock from the mangling at his chest.

"What are you doing up north here?" McComb said, wiping at the facial wounds.

"I came out for gazelle. Silver Wolf asked me—to come in this place. In case I should meet with you."

McComb frowned. "Why? I just left there."

"I have a message for you. The Gypsies have broken camp."

McComb glowered through the thick beard.

"But not all of them. Silver Wolf believes your enemy waits for you—at the original campsite."

McComb nodded.

"Silver Wolf asks you—to take me with you."

McComb sighed heavily. "Lie still, my friend."

"Be watchful. The cougar is still—here somewhere."

McComb scented the air, like an animal might. He thought he had a whiff of a musty pelt, coming from the rocks. He walked to the pinto, and drew the Collier shotgun from its saddle scabbard. Reaching into a saddle wallet, he procured two cartridges and loaded the two-barreled gun. He had to deal with the cougar first.

"I'll be right back," he said in English. He remembered, and repeated it in Shoshoni.

He climbed the hill, and stopped at the edge of the rocks. Cougars were excellent hunters. If the animal was big, and smart enough, the gun might be worthless. The big cat had already shown its disdain for the human animal, and its fearlessness. He had to be careful.

He moved warily into the rocks. His sense of smell and hearing were superior to almost anybody's he had ever encountered, and he was keeping them honed at the moment. The odor of the pelt was definite now, as he moved into the boulders and rocks, and he stopped as he heard a very slight, almost inaudible movement of pebbles up above him. He saw nothing. He moved on, the shotgun out in front, every muscle taut with anticipation.

In a flashing moment, a furry demon hurtled through the air at him from an unseen boulder, yowling as it came.

McComb turned in the same moment his peripheral vision picked up the movement, and his finger squeezed down on the first trigger of the shotgun.

The gun went off in the same instant the cat hit him full in the chest and face. The cougar was jerked sidewise by the impact of the hot lead, then McComb was on his back with the fury of the cat ravaging him, clawing at his chest and belly, trying to rip him up. The cougar was hit in the shoulder, but the lead did not stop it. That wild, primeval face was in McComb's, the yellow eyes blazing hatred, the mouth open with big fangs going for McComb's throat.

McComb had never seen such a large cougar. The animal was full upon him now, raking and biting, him holding it off with the gun, the big cat trying desperately to kill him. The stink of the pelt filled McComb's nostrils, and the long teeth tore at his arm, his gun, his shirt. McComb cocked his leg up and got his right boot into the animal's underside, and he shoved with all his strength. The cougar went flying off him, but for just a split instant. It hit the ground near McComb and then was springing back on him in one motion, growling savagely. McComb just got the gun turned again, and fired for the second time.

This blast hit the cougar full in the face, and tore most of its head off.

The animal hit him again, with the claws still raking, and then it fell off him to his left, jerking and jumping on the ground for a moment. Then it was still.

McComb got up, slowly and painfully. He was cut up on the right arm, the chest, and the left hand. The animal had not gotten to his face. He looked down at the blood on him, and realized the wounds were all rather shallow.

He stared down at the cougar. There was little left of the head, and the left shoulder was chewed up. McComb shook his head, wondering how the cat could have ignored that first hit the way it had. From head to tip of tail, the cat looked as long as a gut wagon to McComb.

McComb turned and wearily moved back down the hill, to where the Shoshoni was still lying in the scrub brush.

"I killed it," he said in Shoshoni as he approached the supine figure on the ground. "We won't have to worry about it coming back at us now. Which way did your mount run off to? If I can find it, we can — "

McComb looked down at the figure again, and the brave's eyes were closed. He knelt over the Shoshoni a second time, and looked more closely at his face. "Hey. Are you all right?"

There was no response. McComb reached down and felt for a pulse at the throat. There was none.

"Son of a bitch," he muttered.

It kept piling up on him. This young man might have gone out of his way to come across McComb and deliver that unimportant message. And the cougar had found him.

"Son of a bitch," he repeated moodily.

It took McComb another hour to bury the brave. He knew that Shoshoni tradition and ceremony had been ignored, but he had done his best under the circumstances. He would have to offer his condolences to Silver Wolf the next time he saw him.

It was midafternoon when McComb got going again, after cleaning up his own wounds. He hurt all through the rest of that day from the beating he had taken in the cougar attack, and he felt very low in spirit. From the time he left Nalin there on that dark night, things had seemed to go wrong. Except for being found by Iron Knife. But even that did not seem like good luck to McComb, now. Maybe, he thought, he would have been better off if Iron Knife had not found him out there on that dusty plain. Maybe it would have been merciful for him to have died there and been eaten by vultures.

No, he finally decided. That would have left Skinner out there alive, to gloat over Nalin's murder, and the way she had been mistreated from the moment they had taken her, that long time ago in his cabin. He could not accept that. Skinner must pay for his crimes against Nalin, McComb's dead friend, and McComb himself. The same with Lazlo. The law had failed to deal with them, what law there was. Now it was up to McComb.

This long day, though, was far from over. Still hurting from the cougar wounds, and hunched into himself emotionally, McComb just wanted to cover some ground and camp close enough to where the

176

Gypsy site had been so he could reach it the following day. But in late afternoon, with the sun heading back down across the yellow sky, he came upon another surprise.

He rounded a curve in the trail, thinking his private thoughts, and suddenly the scene lay before him. There was a small war party of Bannock Indians, six of them, and they had a white man tied to a dead cottonwood tree. They were laughing and raising hell and they had knives out and were starting to cut on him. They had stripped his clothing off except for a pair of long yellowed underwear.

McComb squinted down on the scene, and rode up closer. The figure at the tree looked familiar. He focused on the man again, and recognized Will Beaumont.

It was Beaumont who had brought McComb the news about Nalin, and had given over to McComb the personal articles of Nalin that proved the Camargue Gypsies were holding her. That had all been at the early spring trade fair at Bear Lake, and that seemed like a hundred years ago to McComb now.

One of the Bannocks had turned and seen McComb, and the noise subsided as they all turned to look at him. The local Bannocks knew of McComb, but they were not his friends like the Shoshoni were. They wore buckskin pants and no shirts, and had feathers in their headbands, and red and yellow war paint on their hard-looking faces. Their ponies were picketed nearby, at a smaller tree.

Beaumont had seen McComb now, too, and McComb saw a look of small relief come into his lean, bony face. His hands were tied behind the tree trunk, and his ankles were bound together. There were two long slashes on his chest, one on either side of it, and McComb knew what that meant. They were preparing to flay him, strip the skin away from his body in much the way that McComb would skin a buffalo or beaver. Except that Beaumont was very much alive, and would be through most of the slow process. It was an ugly way to die.

"McComb!" Beaumont said in his throat. His naked chest looked pitifully lean to McComb, and his face gaunt. But McComb knew that Beaumont, a trapper like himself, was tough under that thin frame, and would last a long time.

McComb rode on in toward the group, and dismounted fifteen feet away from them. He made no move toward any of his guns. He could not have killed six of them before they could get to him, anyway. He raised a hand in greeting. The most mature-looking of them came up to McComb arrogantly. He hesitated, then returned the greeting.

"You are the Long Hunter."

McComb nodded. "And you must be Swift Eagle," he said to the Bannock, recognizing the son of a local Bannock chief, and the equivalent in stature to Iron Knife of the local Shoshoni.

The other man nodded. McComb's Bannock had been halting and broken, so Swift Eagle now spoke in English.

"Why do you come here, Long Hunter? You are not a welcome visitor at this place."

"Save me, McComb!" Beaumont called out to him. His voice cracked at the end.

McComb eyed him sidewise. He did not like Will Beaumont. He was a rather unscrupulous fellow who despised most Indians and cheated them and others every chance he got. It was he who had demanded payment from McComb, for giving Mc-Comb the things of Nalin, at the trade fair. He was underhanded, untrustworthy, and dislikable. But he was a white man, and another trapper.

McComb looked back at Swift Eagle. "I come upon you and your brave warriors by chance," he said. "I am on my way to the west, to find a Gypsy camp. Have you come from that way?"

Swift Eagle nodded. He was hard-looking and muscular. His five warriors now all faced McComb with hostility, muttering among themselves. One carried a Plains rifle under his arm.

Swift Eagle nodded again. "We passed by the Gypsies. Two wagons." He spat on the ground with great disdain. "We should have killed them."

McComb thought for a moment. This confirmed what the Shoshoni had told him. Some of the Gypsies had left. The ones who stayed behind, he knew, would be Skinner and Lazlo. And maybe Camargue. They would have stayed hoping McComb would return. Because Skinner wanted to kill McComb almost as much as McComb wanted to kill him.

Almost.

McComb sighed heavily as he looked over toward the sagging Beaumont again. "I know this man, Swift Eagle," he began. "We have done much business together. Are you preparing to kill him?"

"He will die, yes. With great pain and suffering."

"May I ask what violation of Bannock law he has

179

committed to require this undignified death?" Mc-Comb asked him.

A warrior came up to Swift Eagle excitedly, anger in his round face. "Why do you make palaver with this hunter? He must be told to leave us! He may not interfere!"

McComb caught most of the Bannock language remarks, and eyed the warrior balefully. Swift Eagle turned to the other man just as angrily. "I will tell him when to leave! I will speak with him for as long as I believe is necessary!"

The other fellow retreated back to the other four, who stood about looking very surly, as if they would prefer to skin McComb now, over Beaumont.

Swift Eagle turned back to McComb. "Excuse my warriors, they are very angry with this man. He found one of our maidens at a riverbank, by herself. Just this morning. He raped her, beat her, and then slit her throat so she would not speak of his crimes."

McComb's face went very long, and he looked over at Beaumont. Beaumont said nothing, but looked away.

"These are serious matters," McComb said to Swift Eagle.

"They are," the Bannock replied. "And our law decrees a fitting death for him. We will not have you come between this man and his just punishment, Long Hunter."

"I understand," McComb said. "May I speak with him for just a moment?"

The Bannock hesitated. "Go ahead."

McComb walked over to Beaumont. "What the

hell is the matter with you, Beaumont?" he said darkly.

Beaumont ignored the question. "Get me out of this, McComb. I can't die like this. I always feared this kind of thing. I won't be able to take it, McComb! Offer them money! I'll make it up to you!"

McComb felt disgust well up in him. "Did you rape the Bannock girl, damn you? Did you kill her? Don't lie to me."

Beaumont looked into those brooding eyes and knew that McComb would see a lie. He nodded almost imperceptibly. "My God, McComb, she was only a goddamn Indian."

McComb remembered Nalin, and scowled deeply at Beaumont. If Beaumont were not tied up, he would have slugged him. Beaumont saw the anger in McComb's face.

"Oh, hell. I mean—"

"You are a bastard, Beaumont," McComb growled out.

He turned back to Swift Eagle, and the dark faces of his warriors. Beaumont deserved the death penalty. But no criminal deserved the kind of death Beaumont was about to suffer.

"I agree with you, Swift Eagle," he said. "This man must die."

"Good Jesus, McComb!" Beaumont cried out.

"However," McComb went on, "I ask as a friend of the Bannock and Shoshoni that I be allowed to kill him."

Beaumont stared wildly toward McComb for a moment, and then realization came into his face, un-

181

derstanding of what McComb was trying to do for him.

"And how would you end his pitiful life?" Swift Eagle asked.

"I would kill him in an honorable way, with this weapon of war," McComb said, putting his hand on the revolver at his hip.

Swift Eagle shook his head. "That would be an easy end for him, and not what is expected by the Great Spirits."

"What is he saying?" the angry warrior said to Swift Eagle.

"He is a white man," McComb offered. "He ought to be allowed to die by the white man's laws, if possible. I do not think the Great Spirits will be offended."

Swift Eagle hesitated. He knew there were some Bannocks who had great admiration for McComb. He looked toward the angry warrior. "There is a rule that might apply. The dead maiden had no relatives but a sick father, so this warrior here has come to act for him, in avenging the girl's death. He was to do most of the cutting on this killer."

McComb looked over at the stocky Bannock Swift Eagle was referring to, the one who had made the angry remarks.

"If he agrees," Swift Eagle went on, "he may enter into combat with you for the right to kill the trapper. Because you have intervened on the trapper's behalf. But this can happen only if he wants it." He had lapsed into Bannock, because of the complexity of the conversation, but McComb followed most of it.

McComb regarded the warrior briefly. He was big

for an Indian, as tall as McComb and well muscled. "Ask him," McComb told Swift Eagle.

Swift Eagle turned to the warrior and spoke to him in fast Bannock, and the fellow listened intently. There was some muttering among the others when Swift Eagle finished. The angry warrior cast a dark look at McComb, a wild look, and then nodded to Swift Eagle. He figured he would kill McComb, anyway, and then do as he wished with Beaumont.

"He will fight you," Swift Eagle said in English. "It will be with knives."

For a brief moment, McComb wondered why he was risking his life, just to make an ornery bastard's death easier. But he knew that he had to do it, to live with himself later. "Okay," he said.

The Bannock warrior drew a short, slim knife from his pants, where it had rested in a sheath. It already had dried blood on it, from where he had cut Beaumont's chest. He glanced at the dark stains on it, and grinned slightly at McComb. McComb responded by drawing his big Bowie from its leather sheath.

"These are the only weapons that may be used," Swift Eagle said to McComb. "I must take your gun."

McComb looked down at the Patterson-Colt sidearm. Then he reluctantly drew it and gave it over to Swift Eagle. He was now at Swift Eagle's mercy.

"Now you may proceed," Swift Eagle told him.

The Bannock warrior and McComb faced each other, like two brown bears on their hind legs. McComb was weakened somewhat by his captivity with the Gypsies, and his trek in the heat, and by the earlier fight with the cougar. But a weakened McComb was a lot like a weakened grizzly. There was plenty of raw animal power left.

They circled each other. The Bannock slashed out with the slim knife, and McComb jerked backward, and it missed his chest. He feigned with the Bowie, and the Bannock ducked to one side. The Indian was agile, but a little awkward in his movements.

The Bannock was very assured. He passed the knife into his left hand, feinted with it, and punched it back into his right hand. In a flashing movement, he struck out at McComb's belly.

McComb felt a slashing cut through his rawhides, as he arced the Bowie toward the Bannock's chest. It connected below the Indian's shoulder, slicing him there across his bare, bronze skin. He stepped back, grabbing at the shallow wound, and his face revealed a new emotion, that of fear. The arrogance was already gone.

McComb glanced down and saw blood on his clothing, and felt hot, raw pain across his abdomen.

"Shit," he muttered. The warrior was good. He was fast, and he was strong.

They circled each other some more, each looking for an advantage, like boxers. McComb had seen a kick-boxing match once, in a mining camp. The smaller man had been a Frenchman from New Orleans, and he had so bloodied his opponent before they called the fight, so tore him up inside with his feet and hands, that the other man died later. McComb did not want to be that other fellow, here today. He did not want to get cut up so badly that, even if he won, he lost.

He swung the Bowie again, and the razor-sharp blade cut the Bannock's cheek, all the way from his left eye down to his mouth.

The Bannock touched his face, and saw the blood on his hand, and went crazy. He launched himself bodily at McComb, swinging with the slim knife. McComb caught the knife hand with his left one, and then they were hitting the ground together, rolling in the dust, struggling for control. McComb was suddenly on the bottom, with the Bannock over him, and the thin point of the other man's knife was coming down at McComb's left eyeball. The Indian was going to pop his eye, and drive the point of the knife on down into McComb's brain pan. The knife came closer and closer, and the Indian's strength seemed unstoppable. The point was within three inches of McComb's eye, then one inch.

McComb broke free with his right hand, and in a last-strength movement, thrust the Bowie up into the Indian's belly.

The Bannock's eyes saucered, and the knife dropped away from McComb's eye. The thrust of McComb was not fatal, but he knew the Bannock could not live after a disgrace. It was not honorable to let him live. McComb thrust the weapon home, to the hilt, and then rammed it upward toward the Bannock's heart. The eyes saucered even wider, and then the Indian fell off him.

McComb struggled to his feet, bleeding at the abdomen and on the right arm. But both were shallow wounds. He looked down on the fallen Bannock, and the warrior shivered through his body, and died. McComb shook his head slowly. "Hell," he said.

One of the other warriors said something in hot anger to Swift Eagle, but Swift Eagle silenced him. Then he turned to McComb, and handed his revolver back to him.

"You have fought honorably, Long Hunter, and have won. You may have the duty of ending this white man's life."

"I—regret this outcome, Swift Eagle," McComb said.

"The Great Spirits decreed it," the other man told him.

McComb took the revolver in hand and walked over to Beaumont. Beaumont eyed him with fear. "You don't have to do it, McComb," he said. "Ask them to let me go. Tell them you'll turn me over to the law at Fort Bonneville."

McComb looked at him.

"They respect you now. I know these people, I've dealt with them. They'll listen to you now."

Swift Eagle and the other warriors came and stood close around McComb, watching his face.

"I killed a man for you, you son of a bitch," McComb said quietly to Beaumont.

Beaumont licked dry lips. "You killed an Indian. He was trying to kill you, for Christ's sake," he argued desperately. "Are you really going to kill another white man, in cold blood? Because some Indian wants you to?"

McComb regarded him stonily. He raised the revolver and aimed it at Beaumont's forehead.

"You'll roast in hell for this, by God!" Beaumont screamed at him. *"Your soul will fry in Hades!"*

186

"I hope you were worth all this," McComb said grimly.

"You're a goddamn Judas, McComb! A goddamn traitor to the white race! I hope you rot in—"

McComb squeezed the trigger of the Patterson-Colt, and there was a hot explosion that rent the silence, and a blue hole appeared in Beaumont's forehead, between his eyes.

Beaumont's eyes bulged, and his mouth flew open, as if he were going to continue his tirade against McComb. But his jaw worked silently, and no sound issued forth. Beaumont was dead, and it was over.

McComb turned back to Swift Eagle. The tension had drained out of the air, and the faces of his warriors were relaxed now.

"I am indebted to you, Swift Eagle," McComb told him.

"You are an honorable man, Long Hunter," the Indian told him. "And a brave warrior. Justice has been done. The blood appetite of the spirits has been sated."

McComb nodded.

"You must not cut him down," Swift Eagle said. "He must remain here until the birds eat his rotting flesh, and the sun bleaches his evil bones."

McComb looked over at the lifeless Beaumont, and sighed heavily. "All right," he said. He holstered the revolver, and went over to his mount. Swift Eagle followed him over there.

"Why did you do it?" the Indian said soberly to him. "Why did you wish to give any dignity to the end of this man's life?"

McComb thought for a moment. "I don't know," he said.

A few minutes later, he was riding off along the trail, with the Bannocks looking somberly after him.

In the west, the sun was getting low, and McComb would be camping soon for the night, and resting from all of this.

That was something he needed very badly.

Chapter Ten

There was a growing air of tension and unrest in the Camargue camp.

Both Camargue and Lazlo had given up on McComb's returning for Nalin. Camargue had already voiced his interest in pulling up stakes and heading west to join up with his family. Lazlo wanted to get on with Skinner's big plans for raking in capital for them. Lazlo liked to eat well, dress well, and have women available to him. Money could do all that for him, and he wanted to get at it, embark immediately on the stealing and the robbery. Skinner unfolded plans for cracking frontier banks, and robbing stagecoaches. That would mean heading east, and that was just fine with Lazlo. But the trouble was, all Skinner did was talk about it. He was fanatical in his will to have it out with McComb, and in his belief that McComb would return to this place because of the Apache woman.

It was the morning after McComb's encounter with the Bannocks on the trail leading to them, and they had just eaten breakfast and were sitting in the shade of the conestoga-style wagon, drinking chicory coffee out of tin cups. Across the campsite, on the far side of a low fire, was the cage wagon with the canvas covering, where they had kept McComb like an animal. Horses were tethered to a line strung between two small mesquite trees. It was getting close to midmorning, and the sun was warm already.

Lazlo stared across at the cage, and wished they had been able to keep McComb in it until Skinner's arrival. Skinner would have killed McComb, the thing would be behind them, and he and Skinner would be out raising hell by now. Maybe back at Santa Fe or Albuquerque, where there was a kind of civilization, and men carried gold coins in their pockets.

But Skinner wanted to stay, and Skinner usually got what he wanted.

"What do you think, Mule?" he was saying to Skinner on that warm early summer morning. "When we leave here, maybe you and me ought to head east. There's more money laying around, just waiting to be picked up, in civilized places. We don't know what it will be like in California."

Camargue and Skinner both looked over at him. Camargue looked very European sitting there in his corduroy work pants and blouse-sleeved shirt, with a small red leather vest over it. He was not wearing a hat, and his gray hair was wild and unruly this morning. He regarded Skinner balefully.

Skinner looked like a bull, sitting there with his

190

bald head bare to the morning sun. Camargue had never seen so beefy a man. Skinner looked as hard as sacked salt.

"I never had no thought of going to California," Skinner said gratingly. "I like the idea of Santa Fe, too. But before we end up there, I want to hit some gold mining camps on the Colorado. We could come out of that area with bags of the yellow stuff, and be gone before they knew what hit them."

Lazlo grinned. That was the way he liked to hear Skinner talk. "That sounds just fine, Mule," he said. "But—how long are you going to hang around here waiting for that mountain man? You going to set a time limit of some kind?"

Skinner gave him a hard look.

Camargue saw the look, but jumped in, anyway. "I must ask the same question, Skinner. My family waits for me ahead, on the trail to California. They need me with them. In my opinion, if McComb were coming back here, he would be here by now."

"Nobody forced you to set them others loose," Skinner said dryly. "I told you, I need you and these wagons here, for bait. When I'm done with you, you can go."

A small silence filtered across the campsite.

"I think it would be nice if we put some time limit on our stay here," Lazlo ventured.

Skinner hurled a furious look at him. *"I told you, goddamn it! He'll be here!"*

Lazlo averted his gaze from that hostile one.

Skinner threw the end of his coffee onto the ground. He seemed to get himself under better control, as he sat there. "We won't be here forever, don't worry. I ain't spending the rest of my god-damn life in the shade of these mesquites. I ain't no goddamn fool, Lazlo." He looked out across the buffalo grass, to a distant horizon. "But he's com-ing. I can feel it in my bones, like old folks feel the rheumatiz. He's on his way here."

Lazlo sighed. "I sure as hell hope so," he said.

Skinner looked over at him again. "Look at it this way, Lazlo. McComb is a goddamn Indian lover. Some say he's got Indian blood in him. When he finds out what we done to that Apache squaw of his, you think he's just going to let bygones be by-gones? If he come after her before, what do you think he'll do now? That wild man will track us down if he has to go to China to find us. And he won't never quit, he's a goddamn maniac." He looked past Lazlo. "I never seen no man fight like he done with me, when he caught me. He thinks and acts like a goddamn grizzly. You want to keep looking over your back for a thing like that hunting you, for the rest of your miserable life?"

Both Camargue and Lazlo were staring hard at Skinner by the time he finished. For Skinner to talk about another man like that, Skinner the brute, Skinner the animal, Lazlo figured McComb must be something terrible when he was healthy. Lazlo had never seen him any way but wounded, sick, and malnourished. A little knife of fear skittered along Lazlo's spine, realizing that McComb would be after him, too.

"I see what you mean, Mule," he said quietly.

Camargue just sighed heavily. Every day he delayed his departure, his group got farther away, even though they were traveling slowly until he caught up with them. The plan was that they halt at a well-known watering place, if Camargue had not arrived by then, and wait it out for him.

"As for you, Gypsy," Skinner said arrogantly to Camargue, "you quit straddling a fence. You got to get on this with us, you understand? You can't carry water on both shoulders. As long as I'm here, you're here."

Camargue glowered at him. He blamed Lazlo for this, and could not forgive him for bringing this man down upon them. He did not reply to Skinner.

"My best guess is that McComb will be here within—"

Skinner stopped, and listened. A rider was approaching. "Listen," he said.

The three of them rose, and then they spotted the lone rider coming in toward their camp. He came openly, and rather swiftly. Skinner took the Navy 1843 revolver from its holster, and stood awaiting the arrival of the stranger. Lazlo rested his right hand on his Tranter sidearm.

The rider came right on into camp, and he was a young man. He rode well, but he was dressed more like an Easterner than a cowboy or rancher.

"Morning, gentlemen," he said with a smile. "Mind if I rest my mount?"

Skinner looked him over. He looked like a greenhorn. Skinner wondered if he had anything to steal.

He looked past him, and saw no other riders. "Why not?" he said.

The young fellow dismounted.

"Can I offer you a cup of chicory?" Lazlo said, falling in with Skinner's hospitality.

"Thanks," the rider said.

Camargue got the coffee, and handed a cup to the young man, studying his face closely. The other man sipped it, and smiled. "Good," he said. "We ran out three days ago."

Skinner eyed him narrowly. "We?"

The fellow nodded. "I'm from a two-wagon train, just three miles or so behind you out of Fort Bonneville. We were told there was a water hole up here somewhere. I came out looking for it."

Skinner looked in the direction of Fort Bonneville, and exchanged a look with Lazlo. "There ain't no water around here," he said.

"I think there is a stream several miles ahead," Camargue put in.

Skinner gave him a look.

"Well, since I'm here," the fellow went on, "I wonder if you might have a horse to sell. One of ours went lame. We could also use some flour, if you have any to spare. We can pay you good for it."

Skinner glanced again at Lazlo. "Why, I think we can spare some flour. Maybe we could even sell you that old mare over there. Right, Camargue?" he added meaningfully.

Camargue hesitated. "Maybe," he said.

"How far off did you say those wagons are?" Lazlo said.

The young man looked at him. "About three miles. Maybe less," he said. "Incidentally, my name is Atwood. There's six of us, two families headed for California."

"You got some haul ahead of you," Lazlo said.

Atwood nodded. "We know. But we got us our dreams, and we mean to see they come true. We don't care how hard it might be."

Skinner grunted in his throat. "You say you got money to pay for a horse and a load of flour?"

Atwood grinned. "Sure have. You can rest easy on that score. But that's back at our wagons, of course."

Skinner thought a moment. "Tell you what, we'll sell you the things you want. Lazlo and me will take the horse back there ourselves, but we want you to stay put here till we get back. We been watching out for a Shoshoni war party, and we don't want to leave the old man here alone."

Atwood hesitated. "Why, sure."

"We'll get paid on that end for everything, and then when we get back, you can haul the flour back on your mount. Is that okay?"

"Sounds just dandy to me," Atwood told him. "It suits me right down to the ground."

Skinner smiled a hard smile. "Fine. Now, what do you think that mare over there is worth?"

They talked price over the next few minutes, and finally the bargaining was over. Skinner and Lazlo saddled up their mounts, and advised Atwood they would be right back, and carried a note away with them with Atwood's signature at the end of it, stating the sale prices.

"They always send their best man out scouting for them," Skinner said to Lazlo after they were out of earshot of the Gypsy camp. "I figured we'd keep him out of it till we got what we wanted."

"I'm with you, Mule," Lazlo told him.

"When they pay us, you watch where they go to get the money," Skinner said.

They saw the wagons on the horizon in just a short time, and rode up there quickly with the third horse on a tether behind them, an animal they fully intended to take back with them. Skinner thought of just shooting Atwood and then not having to go through this charade, but he wanted to be convinced these people had enough to kill for.

They were greeted with curious looks from the people at the wagons when they rode in. There was another young man, a rather thin fellow. There were also two women in long, gingham dresses, a boy in his early teens, and a girl who looked about ten. When Lazlo reported where the other man of their group was, and showed them his note, they all relaxed some, but the women continued to cast wary looks at Skinner.

Skinner and Lazlo had dismounted, and picketed all the animals to a nearby sapling. Skinner looked around. The two wagons were typical conestogas, or prairie schooners, and they looked as if they had cost plenty. Skinner liked that.

"Well, I see you people are all outfitted for a long trip," he said to them in the gruff voice.

"That's right," the young man replied. "We read about how green those valleys are in California, and how rich the soil. We just gave up everything, our two families, and headed west."

"Sounds like a smart move," Lazlo put in.

"Can I offer you something to drink?" the closest woman asked. Both women were rather plain looking, and quiet. "I just made some lemonade, from lemons we picked up at Fort Bonneville."

"Why, don't mind if we do," Lazlo said with a grin.

Skinner gave him a quick look, but went along. "Sure, we can take a short spell before riding back," he said.

They all sat around a burned-out fire on camp chairs, and the women brought them lemonade in real glasses. Skinner shook his head slowly. He had not had anything like this since he was a kid. He almost asked for a drink of whiskey instead, but thought better of it.

All three adults sat with Skinner and Lazlo, and the boy and girl moved over to a wagon, and began peeling some potatoes from the train's supplies.

"Where are you all from?" Lazlo said, as he and Skinner and the young man drank lemonade.

"Oh, we're from Ohio originally," the young fellow said. His name, it turned out, was Jameson. "But we holed up in Kansas through this last winter. We hope to get to California before this summer is out."

"Are you a farmer, Jameson?" Skinner asked, still looking about to assay the wealth of this group.

"Oh, no. Atwood has done some farming. But I worked in a general store. No, we'll have to start new careers out in California. We expect to set up an outfitting store for the miners, somewhere around the Feather River. There's talk of a lot of gold in the ground around there."

"I guess that would take quite some capital, wouldn't it?" Skinner said, trying to keep the excitement out of his voice.

"Well, we both had a nest egg saved up," Jameson said. "We just have to hope it's enough, when we get out there."

Skinner nodded, and swigged the rest of the lemonade. Lazlo did likewise, feeling a tension mount inside him. "Well, that's real good lemonade," he said.

"It sure is," Skinner said. "And we thank you, ladies, for the refreshment." He rose, and they all did. "Now, I guess we'll take our pay and light out of here. We don't want to leave Atwood back there all day." He grinned.

The two women took the empty glasses back, and then Jameson excused himself and went into the nearest wagon. Lazlo could hear him rummaging around in there, getting into a trunk. He peered into the end of the vehicle, and watched Jameson take some gold coins from a cloth bag, and put the bag back into the trunk. Skinner was telling the homeliest of the women how much he admired her lemonade. Jameson came back out with the money.

"Well, this is it," he said, handing the money over to Skinner. "And we sure appreciate your parting with the flour, and particularly the horse."

Skinner looked down at the gold coins, and a small fever welled up in him. His face changed, and became hard and sober. Lazlo saw the change, and rested his hand on his revolver.

"I guess you got a lot of this in there, huh?" Skinner said to Jameson.

The women were standing nearby, and the children had stopped with their chores, and were watching, too.

Jameson studied Skinner's face closely. "Why, like I told you. We got some capital between us. It's not a lot," he said carefully, "but it might give us a little start when we get out there."

Skinner nodded. "You got it in both wagons, I guess?"

Jameson's mouth suddenly began going dry. "How would that matter to you, Mister Skinner? You have your money."

Skinner hauled off and slugged Jameson across the face with a backhand blow that almost knocked him out. Jameson fell hard to the ground, dazed and bleeding at the mouth.

Behind him, his wife began screaming loudly. The other woman was now wailing, and the little girl across the camp began crying, too.

"Shut up," Skinner said to the screaming woman.

She kept screaming. He drew the Derringer Navy .54 and shot her in the chest.

The woman jumped backward and hit the ground hard. She was dead when she hit.

"Oh, my God!" the dazed Jameson said dully, seeing his lifeless wife on the ground. "Oh, good Jesus!"

The small girl began yelling loudly now, and the second woman acted as if she were going to faint at any moment. "Oh, God have mercy on us," she muttered.

"Stop that kid from yelling!" Skinner said angrily.

The woman went to the girl, who was her daughter. The boy, a Jameson, stared bug-eyed at his mother on the ground, with the crimson hole in her chest. The woman put her arms around both of them, looking very white and faint.

"Now you tell her," Skinner said to Jameson, and waving the thick revolver toward the second woman, "to go show my friend here where all of your money is."

The other man looked back at his wife, and knew that she was dead. "Goddamn you!" he said quietly.

"You tell her!" Skinner warned him.

While Jameson hesitated, the teen-age boy suddenly broke from the woman's arms, and went for a rifle affixed to the wooden side of the conestoga they were at. Lazlo saw the movement first. Just as the boy reached the gun, Lazlo fired and hit the boy in the back. The boy grabbed at himself, then slid to the ground, leaving a smear of blood on the wood.

"Oh, God!" the woman, who was Atwood's wife, cried out.

Jameson was stunned. "My wife. My son," he said numbly.

"Maybe you didn't hear me," Skinner said in a growl.

Jameson looked at him as if he must be insane. He rose awkwardly to his feet. He turned weakly to the Atwood woman. "Show him," he said almost inaudibly. Then he went and knelt over his wife, and took her head in his hands. "Oh, Holy Father," he mumbled over her. "My dear Sarah."

The Atwood woman left her daughter, terror-stricken, and went to the back of the wagon. She pointed inside it. "The wooden box," she said. "It's—not locked."

Lazlo went inside, and in a moment came out with the box. He opened it up in front of Skinner, and his face brightened. There were a lot of gold and silver coins inside.

"Now the other wagon," Skinner commanded the woman.

She went and pointed out the trunk where the first coins had come from. "There. Take it all. But please don't kill any more. I ask you in the name— of God."

Lazlo went inside and then came out with the bag of coins. This time they were all gold. There were a lot of them. He showed the bag to Skinner.

Skinner grinned widely. "Well, well," he said. "Looks like our day, my boy."

Lazlo went and stashed the stuff in his saddle-bags, and they were heavy when he was through. Skinner took a good look at the Atwood woman and decided she was not worth their attention. The party was almost over.

"Now, you come over behind that wagon with me," Skinner said to Jameson. "Lazlo, you see that this lady and her kid don't cause no trouble."

Lazlo nodded.

"Please. Don't kill any more of us," the Atwood woman said. "Let my husband come back to me." She clutched the little girl tightly.

"You just move along with me," Skinner said to Jameson.

Jameson hesitated, then followed orders. They went around to the far side of the nearest wagon, and there was a brief silence back there, as Lazlo listened. Then a shot rang out.

"Oh, no!" the Atwood woman moaned.

Skinner had put a bullet in Jameson's head back there, casually, as if he were slaughtering a cow. He came back into the compound now, his gun still smoking.

"Now why don't you just give me that little girl for a minute?" Skinner said to her.

Lazlo looked at him quizzically. He had been sure he would let the Atwood woman and her young daughter live. "What are you going to do?" he said quietly to Skinner.

Skinner eyed him darkly. "What do you think?"

Lazlo licked dry lips. He had had ideas about killing Nalin, before Skinner arrived. But that was a squaw. This was a white woman, and a little girl. Lazlo had been rather shocked when Skinner had killed the Jameson woman, just to silence her.

"Is that necessary?" Lazlo said.

The girl and the woman were both crying now. The woman was also trembling visibly, and the girl was clutching her mother's waist, hiding her face.

Skinner regarded Lazlo with an impatient look. "You want witnesses to this?" he growled out.

Lazlo swallowed hard. "I — guess not."

"Use your head," Skinner told him. "You act like you got clabber for brains."

Lazlo said nothing. Skinner went over to the woman, and saw that she would not release her daughter without a fuss. His patience had run out. "Well, lady, I thought I'd do it so it would be easier for you. Now you don't give me no choice."

"Take our wagons!" the woman blurted out hysterically. "Take everything! I'll — even go with you!"

Skinner grinned, and shook his head. "Not hardly, lady." He raised the .54 revolver and squeezed the trigger and there was a violent explosion. The side of her head blew away.

As she slid to the ground, the girl began screaming loudly. Skinner fired again, shutting the noise off as if a door had been closed on it. The two lay together in a heap, at his feet. He holstered the gun.

"I'd say this was a big day for us," he said to Lazlo.

Lazlo looked at Skinner differently. He was not as sure he wanted to ride with him, as he had been before. "Yeah, Mule. A big day."

"Now we'll ride back with all this gold, and make Camargue's eyes bulge." Skinner grinned, showing no feeling at all about what he had just done. "But we'll shoot that other greenhorn first thing."

"Right, Mule," Lazlo said somberly.

They went to their mounts, and Skinner checked Lazlo's saddlebags to make sure the gold and silver were secure, then they both released their tethers and mounted their horses. Skinner turned to Lazlo.

"You know, I ain't half as mad at that mountain man now," he said, his little eyes glittery. "In fact, if he don't show up pretty soon, I'll let the old man get going. I don't need to kill him no more. He ain't worth it. There's too much gold out there, just waiting for me to take it."

Lazlo nodded doubtfully. "I know what you mean, Mule."

"Okay, let's get back. But we won't ride directly to the Camargue wagons. We'll do a little detour, to try to throw anybody off that wants to follow us."

Lazlo sighed. "Good idea."

Skinner pulled a small Shoshoni headdress from a pocket, a thing he had purchased at Fort Bridger. He threw it on the ground. "There. That ought to make it look like the Indians done this. Come on, let's ride out of here."

Lazlo was amazed at Skinner's cunning. As they passed the far side of the nearest wagon, he looked down at the dead Jameson. Half of his face was blown away, and there were green blowflies already buzzing around the body.

Lazlo followed Skinner out of the camp, then. He had almost forgotten what it was like to ride with Emmett Skinner.

This had been a graphic reminder.

It was something Lazlo would not soon forget.

At about that same moment three miles away, McComb reined in his mount, and shaded his eyes with his hand. Yes, he had been right. There were two wagons out there, the remaining ones of the Gypsy camp. One of them was the cage he had been kept in like an animal.

Something settled hard inside McComb. The bastard Lazlo was probably with those wagons. The man who had starved him and almost killed him, and treated Nalin like a draft animal for all that time. And Skinner was undoubtedly there, too. The monster who had killed McComb's friend, kidnapped his woman, and then killed her when he caught up with the Gypsy train. Because McComb was certain, in his gut, that it was Skinner who had murdered Nalin. Iron Knife had reported it that way, and he had had a good look at what had happened.

McComb checked the ammunition in his revolver, and then pulled the long Sharps 1848 rifle from its saddle scabbard. He checked to see that it, too, was loaded, and then spurred the pinto onward, spitting out a thin cigar he had been chewing on.

He was ready for them.

Almost a mile away, Camargue stared out across the bright, heat-wavering landscape and saw the lone rider out there. His eyes were still excellent, and he recognized the figure after just a brief moment of staring at it.

"Holy Spirit!" he whispered to himself. "It is McComb!"

The greenhorn Atwood had been drinking another cup of coffee at Camargue's fire, entirely unaware that his whole group now lay dead three miles away. He had just looked across the dry terrain for the fifth time, hoping to get some view of Skinner and Lazlo returning.

"What is it?" he said to Camargue.

"You recall our telling you of hostile Shoshonis," Camargue said, thinking quickly. "Well, there is a white man who is part Shoshoni, and he is coming now, see out there?"

"Yes," Atwood said slowly.

"He will have a war party waiting somewhere. When he comes to us, we must kill him."

"Huh?" Atwood said. He did not even have a gun.

Camargue went to the nearby wagon and retrieved two old rifles. He gave one to Atwood. "We have no choice, it will be him or us," he said. "Do you understand? He will also find your family."

Atwood licked dry lips. "I see."

"Go hide behind that other wagon. When he

comes into camp, kill him. Do not hesitate, or he will surely kill you."

Atwood's face had gone long and sober. "I will."

"I will be over here, and between us, we should be able to surprise him," Camargue said.

"You can count on me," Atwood said quietly.

Camargue quickly looked out in the direction of Atwood's wagons, and saw nothing. It appeared there was no chance that Skinner and Lazlo would get back in time. Turning back toward McComb, he saw that the mountain man was now within a quarter-mile of them, and coming on at a steady pace.

Atwood had gone and hidden behind the conestoga-type wagon, and Camargue went and squatted behind the cage wagon. In the middle of the camp, a low fire crackled and sputtered. Out on the plain somewhere, a bird cried raucously.

McComb was within a hundred yards, suddenly. Fifty yards.

Out on the pinto, McComb reined in and stopped his mount. There was a glare of sun on the wagons, and he could not see as well as he would have liked to. He had expected to see movement in the camp by now, but there was none. He had hoped Skinner would show himself first, and that McComb would be able to find him in the sights of the long gun. But at this moment, there was nothing. No sight of people, no sound.

McComb smelled danger.

He nudged the pinto, and began circling the camp. In just a couple of moments, he saw that there were only a couple of horses there, one dray animal and one saddled mount. That surprised him. He came in closer.

At the wagons, Atwood panicked, and rose into sight and fired quickly at McComb.

McComb felt the hot lead tug at his collar. At the same moment, he saw the head and torso of Atwood sticking above the end gate of the wagon. He raised the Sharps and fired from the hip, in one movement, and hit Atwood in the right eye. The slug exploded through Atwood's head like a hot poker, and blew off the crown of his skull.

Atwood went tripping backward, the rifle flying from his grasp, and then he hit in high weeds on his back. His left leg kicked at the ground once, and it was over.

Camargue fired once now, from under the cage wagon, and the bullet kicked up dirt just in front of McComb's mount. McComb dismounted and ran in toward the camp in a wide circle. Camargue, sweating now behind the wagon, fired again, and dug up more dirt, at McComb's feet this time. McComb returned fire after reloading the Sharps, and cracked wood beside Camargue's head. Camargue panicked, and got up and ran for cover of a small cottonwood tree, fifty yards away from camp.

McComb dropped the Sharps, drew the Patterson-Colt, and steadied the sidearm on his knee. He fired at Camargue on the run, and Camargue went down.

McComb knelt in high grass, waiting. There appeared to be no more movement at camp. He rose slowly, and walked into the camp area. He saw Atwood, sprawled on the ground. He entered the campsite, and the horses were rearing nervously. He walked on through it, looking in the Gypsy wagon. Then he went on through the camp and walked over to Camargue.

Camargue was lying on his side, grimacing in raw pain. He had been hit in the side, and was bleeding badly. His dark eyes had a glazed look in them. McComb came and stood over him, looking wild and dangerous.

"Don't — kill me," Camargue gritted out, holding a hand to his side. Blood seeped between his fingers.

"Why not, you son of a bitch?" McComb growled through his dark beard.

"I — saved your life," Camargue hissed out. "I delayed — the decision about killing you."

"You're a goddamn angel from heaven, Camargue," McComb said acidly to him. "Now tell me. Where are they?"

"Who?" Camargue said, stalling.

McComb aimed the revolver at Camargue's head. "You think I'm playing games, old man?"

Camargue saw the deadly purpose in McComb's flashing eyes. "All right. If I tell you, will you spare me?"

"Maybe," McComb told him.

Camargue grunted in pain. "Skinner and Lazlo rode out that way," he said, pointing toward the Atwood-Jameson wagons. "There's a couple of families out there three miles or so. Skinner planned to rob them."

McComb looked over toward the fallen Atwood. "That was one of them?"

Camargue nodded.

"You are a bastard, Camargue," McComb said. "When did they leave here?"

"A couple of—hours ago."

McComb squinted out toward the other encampment. There were no riders in sight out there. He turned back to Camargue, hesitated, and holstered the Patterson-Colt.

"You're a lucky Gypsy, Camargue," he said in the low, hard voice.

Camargue looked up at him. If McComb had looked wild before, it was nothing to the aura of bestial violence that hung over him at this moment. Camargue had never seen him in full possession of his physical power, and it was utterly frightening to him.

Camargue did not reply. He did not feel it was safe to do so.

McComb turned on his heel, and walked back out to his stallion, retrieving the Sharps on the way. He replaced it to its scabbard, mounted the pinto, and rode off in the direction of the other camp.

If the Gypsy were not lying, it would not be long now.

And this time, it would be him or them.

Chapter Eleven

Because of their circuitous route back to the Gypsy encampment, though, Skinner and Lazlo missed McComb completely. While he was still on his way to the Atwood-Jameson wagons, they arrived at the Gypsy camp from the other direction.

Skinner had taken them over rocks and hard ground, to try to make their trail hard to follow, for anyone wanting to find the perpetrators of the Atwood-Jameson killings.

Now, approaching the Gypsy camp slowly, Skinner's eyes narrowed down and a sober look came onto his beefy face.

"What the hell," he said.

Lazlo reined in beside him. "What is it?"

"Something is wrong here," Skinner said, drawing his Derringer slowly.

Lazlo drew his gun, too. "I see what you mean. Where the hell is Camargue?"

"That's what we're going to find out," Skinner said.

They rode on in, slowly. Then Lazlo spotted the body of Atwood, lying in the high weeds.

"Look!" he said.

Skinner saw the body. He looked around them carefully. Then he rode on over to the body.

"McComb," he grated out. "It was McComb."

They both dismounted, still holding the handguns. Skinner inspected the corpse of Atwood, and then went and found Camargue. Camargue made a muffled greeting to them, but now he was dying.

"Son of a bitch," Skinner said. Not for Camargue. Because he had missed the mountain man.

Lazlo bent over Camargue. "Was it McComb?" he said.

Camargue nodded. "Yes," he muttered.

"Son of a bitch," Skinner said. "I don't believe it."

Lazlo looked around the camp, hoping McComb was gone.

"If he was here, you'd be dead," Skinner said to him.

They holstered their guns.

"Why the hell didn't you keep him here?" Skinner suddenly raged at Camargue. "You stupid old man!"

Camargue was going fast. "He—was deadly."

"Where did he go?" Skinner said loudly.

"After you," Camargue said with some small satisfaction. "To that other camp."

"You sent him there?" Skinner said incredulously.

Camargue smiled.

"Shit," Lazlo said. "Let's just get out of here, Mule. You said it, it don't matter now. Look at the gold we got."

Skinner caught his gaze. "It ain't the same now," he said. "He's back. He's looking for us. Just like I thought he would."

"We can still ride out," Lazlo told him.

"Two of us run from one goddamn trapper?" Skinner said in his grating voice. "What kind of a yellow belly are you, goddamn it, Lazlo?"

Lazlo eyed him. "I just mean, we got capital now. We can use it to raise us some hell. What do we need a gunfight for? I don't care if that hunter lives to be a hundred. It won't bother me none."

"Well, it will bother him if you do," Skinner said evenly. "He's over there at the greenhorn camp right now, too, eyeing what we done there. Even if he was to quit chasing us, he's a goddamn witness now. He knows we was there."

Camargue let out a long, ugly rattle from his throat, and died there on the ground. They both looked at him for a long moment.

"He's gone," Lazlo said.

Skinner nodded. "You see what kind of crazy man that trapper is? He come in here and just started shooting. You think we can just walk away from him, and he'll disappear? Like hell, he will.

213

We got to kill him, Lazlo. We ain't got no choice, at this point."

"It just don't ever seem to end," Lazlo said heavily.

"It will end with his goddamn last breath," Skinner told him.

Lazlo nodded slowly. "Yeah."

Skinner walked back into camp, and sat down on a camp stool that had been used by Atwood earlier. Lazlo came and sat near him. Lazlo watched his muscle-crowded face.

"I bet he'll quit chasing us around now," Skinner said. "He knows there's both of us over here, and we know he's over there. He figures he's lost any element of surprise."

"That makes sense," Lazlo said.

"So he'll stay put there," Skinner said.

"He might."

Skinner looked out over the grassland. "In case I got it figured wrong, we'll hole up here for a few hours, and see what happens. Load up all our guns. Rest up. If he don't come by the end of day, we'll go after him."

"Why not just wait him out?" Lazlo suggested, watching Skinner's face. "Make him eventually come to us. Make him take all the chances."

"I waited in that stink bog at Devil's Hole for more time than I can count," Skinner said. "I ain't got it in me to wait much longer. I want this over with. If he ain't come by sundown, we'll go after him. Under the cover of dark."

214

Lazlo nodded uncertainly. "Okay, Mule. In the dark."

Three miles away, McComb was just riding up to within shouting distance of the other encampment.

The first sound he heard upon his arrival there was the loud buzzing of blowflies. Then he saw the vultures that had begun to circle overhead.

He had the Sharps out again, and he expected to be ambushed by Skinner and Lazlo. But he realized rather quickly that there was nobody there. Nobody alive.

After checking the place out visually, he rode on in. The sound of flies was loud now, and he saw the corpse of Jameson first. Then, in past the wagons, he saw the women, and the kids.

"I'll be a son of a bitch," he said under his breath.

It had to be Skinner and Lazlo. He had not thought that even they were capable of this. He dismounted heavily. He walked among the bodies, to make sure they were all dead.

"If that bastard don't go to hell," he said to himself, "there ain't no use in having one."

He made sure they were not hiding in the wagons. Out on the campsite, he found the Shoshoni article dropped by Skinner, and shook his head. He picked it up and stuffed it into his belt.

"It seems like there's a lot of burying going on lately," he said to the corpses. He pulled a shovel off his mount's irons, and went outside of the camp and started digging a common grave for them. The sun was hot, and he did a lot of sweating. As he dug, he remembered the aftermath of the massacre at Goliad. Santa Anna had ordered mass graves to be dug, and McComb's parents had been thrown into such a grave without ID or ceremony.

The horror of those few days at Goliad had stayed in McComb's head permanently. The Mexicans had just left the children there to fend for themselves, when the army moved on, but a neighbor of the McCombs had found McComb and his sister Megan, and taken them in. Not long thereafter, they had all gone west, to try to get to Santa Fe where the neighbor expected financial help from a relative. But they never made it. The whole bunch took down with the prairie fever, and they all succumbed, one by one, except for McComb. His own sister died in his arms, and that had been almost unbearable, after losing both parents. He had been alone out on the prairie then, and very sick, and would have died himself. But he had been found by Apaches, and taken in, and ancient herbs were used on him to make him well.

Now all this reminded McComb forcefully of those ugly days of his youth, when everything that he loved had been taken from him. He dug this grave now, in the heat of the sun, and remembered.

"Listen to me, son," his father had told him, just before he took his place before the firing squad, with Rachel. "They'll pay for this. Nobody gets away with something like this. You remember that. Remember that men can be treacherous. But that, in the long haul, good men prevail over evil ones. Are you listening to me?"

A nod of the head, a scared look. Tears welling in the eyes. "Yes."

"Now, be a brave boy, and take care of your sister. Do you hear me?"

"Yes, Father."

They had dragged Obadiah away from him then, and he and little Megan had been restrained by soldiers while the firing squad did its ugly work. When Megan saw her mother go down, she had begun screaming loudly, and McComb had had to keep her quiet so the soldiers would not kill her.

McComb had come away from that, and later the death of Megan, a very bitter youngster. The Apaches had noticed it in him as soon as he began recovering in their care. In fact, if it had not been for their nurturing of him, he would probably have become an outcast from the world of men and a hater of the human race, he figured. As it was, he became a loner that even the Apaches never fully understood, and he made himself tough, physically and mentally, to prepare, subconsciously, for another Santa Anna. He had taken on the ways of the Indians, too, and that made him seem different and rather wild to white folks. Some thought he did not put much value on human life, but that could not have been further from the truth.

When McComb had heard, later, that Santa Anna's troops had been decimated at San Jacinto, by Houston's small army, he had gone off by himself and let the deep satisfaction seep into him, and had sent a prayer of thanks up to the Apache gods that he figured had helped wreak vengeance on the wicked Mexicans.

By late afternoon, the wide grave was dug, and McComb was dusty and weary. He then went and got the bodies, one by one, and laid them to rest in the rather shallow grave, and last of all covered them with dirt.

Almost immediately the blowflies were gone, and the vultures just disappeared as if they had never been there. The campsite seemed almost peaceful to McComb then. Except that there were small evidences of what had happened. A bloodstain here, a scuffed place there.

Besides the two wagons with their belongings, there were two mules picketed nearby that had been witness to the killings, and which now stood hungry and bewildered on their picket ropes. McComb went over to them and gave them some assurance, speaking to them softly, in the Apache way. He untethered them, one at a time, and gave them a pat on the flank, and they trotted off for a small distance, keeping together.

"At least you can fend for yourselves now," he said. "And you won't get caught in any cross fire."

His mount still stood quietly nearby, grazing on long grass at the edge of the camp. McComb took it and led it fifty yards away from camp, to a low-growing mesquite, and picketed it there.

McComb figured he would wait here for Skinner. If he knew anything about Skinner, Skinner would know now that McComb was there to kill him. And, being an impatient and not altogether intelligent fellow, Skinner would bring Lazlo and come for McComb here, if McComb waited him out.

That would give him a small advantage he had not enjoyed when he rode up to the Gypsy encampment. They would be coming to him, and as the Apaches had taught him, it is best to defend when you are outnumbered, rather than attack.

Of course, he would not know when Skinner was coming, if he came. Nor where he would come from.

McComb went to his saddle wallet, on the pinto's gear, and took out a half-dozen beaver traps he had brought along for just this purpose. He had purchased them at Fort Bridger, when he got his mount and gear back. In the next hour, he took four of them about thirty yards away from camp, in the opposite direction of the Gypsy camp, and set them in high grass, ready to spring if stepped on. Then he took the other two, and set them the same distance away, in the direction of Camargue's camp. Directly in line with any approach from that direction. He hid all of them well, with grass and dirt.

He then went to a saddlebag and took out a dozen mess knives, bone-handled tools with five-inch blades. Going back out to the area of the traps, he buried each knife in the hard soil, handle down, with the blade sticking up into the air. He placed them strategically between the traps, eight on the far side of camp, and four on the near side to the Gypsy camp.

That was Apache, too.

He surveyed his work. At a distance of ten feet, you could not see the traps. In hard sunlight. If Skinner came at dusk, or in the night, they would be invisible at any range.

Now McComb returned to his pinto and took the Collier double-barreled shotgun from its irons, and loaded it carefully. He also stuck several more cartridges into a belt purse at his waist. He walked back into camp slowly, figuring he was ready. He found some coffee in the belongings of the Atwood wagon, built a low fire, and made a pot. He also ate some beef jerky and hardtack, sitting there by the crackling fire.

The sun lowered in the sky.

He watched the horizon.

Down south and west of those two encampments, Ranko had made camp on the banks of a shallow stream. He had wanted to keep going, and not be concerned with when Camargue caught them. But Madame Camargue and Kitta thought they should hole up here, where there was good water, and wait for Camargue. The women had prevailed.

They were three days out from the Camargue camp, and on the far edge of Shoshoni territory, one day north and west of Silver Wolf's village. Ranko realized they were near a couple of Shoshoni villages, and that was one reason he wanted to move on. But Madame was afraid her husband, the chief of their group, would never find them if they traveled too far ahead of him.

Now that the authority of Camargue and Idranyi had been taken away from the group, the boy Vali had become boisterous, troublesome, and generally a nuisance. He cared little what Kitta wanted or demanded, and caused them all inconvenience and frayed nerves. He considered himself one of the men of the family now, and he did about as he pleased. Ranko was not strong enough to take charge of him, and Kitta did not really care anymore. So the boy complained continuously, refused to help with chores, and argued with everybody.

Kitta was so glad to be rid of Skinner that she just went along with Madame in everything, and took little interest in what happened to the family.

Madame was really the one who was holding

the group together. She had always been a strong woman, and now she took charge for her husband. Neither she nor any of them had any idea that Camargue was dead, and that McComb had killed him.

Kitta and Madame Camargue were fixing an evening meal for the group that afternoon when McComb was busy burying the Atwoods and Jamesons, back there at that bloody encampment. Ranko was studying a rough-drawn map of the area, and trying to figure out exactly how many miles they had put between themselves and their old camp. Vali was playing with an old, empty rifle that Ranko had brought with them. Ranko would not allow the boy to have any ammunition for it, however.

It was Vali who saw the Indian first. He looked across the plain, out from the camp, and spotted the lone rider as he was mock-shooting with the rifle.

It was a small Shoshoni boy, riding a paint mare. He must be several years younger than me, Vali thought, as he watched the child approach them warily. It was pleasing to Vali that the Shoshoni boy was younger and smaller than he himself, and that he was merely an Indian. Vali became very excited very quickly.

"Hey! Look what's coming to visit us!" he shouted at Ranko and Madame.

Ranko looked up, from where he sat on a camp stool near a wagon, and so did Madame and

222

Kitta, who were also in the compound formed by the wagons and their tethered horses.

"It is a Shoshoni boy," Ranko announced.

They all stood and watched the boy ride right into their camp. In a moment he was there, still astride his bareback mount. He was part of a hunting party that was just out of sight to the north, a party from Silver Wolf's village, and led by Iron Knife. The boy was the son of one of the hunters.

Vali looked beyond the boy, into the open country. "He's all alone!" he said loudly.

The Shoshoni regarded them sternly. "You are in our territory," he said in a rather high voice. He was a nice-looking boy, well-built, but only eight years old. He wore a feather in his black hair. "You cannot camp on the land of our ancestors."

"He's talking that Indian gibberish," Vali said arrogantly. "What did he say?"

"I think he does not like it that we are camped here," Ranko said.

Madame and Kitta were looking him over. "He is a nice-looking boy," Madame said appraisingly.

"Why is he out here by himself?" Kitta wondered.

The boy saw that they were paying no attention to him. He dismounted from the pony, and frowned at the nearest of them, who was Vali.

"You must leave! The Spirits will be angry!"

Ranko and Madame closed in on the boy. But he exhibited no fear at all. Vali laughed loudly and offensively, and aimed the rifle at him. "Keep up with that coyote talk, and I'll blow your head off, Shoshoni!"

"Vali, put that gun down," Ranko said. "He will think it is loaded."

"I want him to think so," Vali retorted happily.

Ranko came and took the rifle from Vali, and Vali yelled at him. "Hey! You can't do that! I'm defending the family!"

"Shut up, Vali," Kitta said.

"He would bring a fine price from the Bannocks," Madame said.

"Yes," Ranko agreed. "It has been some time since we have had a live Indian to trade away. We could get enough to take us all the way to California. Look at how healthy he appears. They will make a fine slave of him."

Vali walked up to the Shoshoni belligerently. "You see how dumb you are, Indian? Walking right in here like that? Now you're going to bring us a lot of money!"

He had spoken loudly right into the smaller boy's face, and suddenly the Shoshoni drew a hunting knife from its sheath, and wielded it in front of him.

Vali jumped backward a step, then felt foolish. "Did you see that? He wants to kill me!"

"You must leave now!" the Shoshoni boy insisted. But now he looked quickly over his shoulder, to see if he could spot any of the hunters. There were two specks on the horizon, and he relaxed inside.

The others had not seen the riders coming.

"Give me the gun, and I'll kill him!" Vali yelled.

Ranko went around in back of the boy, grabbed his arms, and disarmed him. The knife fell to the ground, and Madame picked it up. The boy struggled fiercely, but Ranko was able to hold him. "See? He is a fine specimen," Ranko said to Madame.

"I don't like this," Kitta said. "We don't need any trouble. Let's let him go."

Vali came up to the Shoshoni, seeing him helpless, and punched the smaller boy hard in the face. The boy reacted painfully, but did not cry out. Blood appeared on his mouth.

"Vali, stop that!" Ranko said. "Here, Madame, help me bind the boy's feet."

The Shoshoni fell to the ground, and Ranko tied his feet with a rope brought by Madame. Madame bent over him. "Yes, he will bring a nice fee. You must quit struggling, boy, or we won't feed you tonight."

Vali came up and kicked the boy viciously in the side. The boy hissed out in pain, but still would not cry out.

"You damnable child!" Ranko said loudly. "Keep away from this Indian. Don't you understand we want him in perfect shape for the trade?"

"You can't tell me what to do with him!" Vali yelled back at Ranko. "You're not the chief! I'm

225

the grandson, I'm in charge here! I'll do what I—"

He stopped in midsentence, and they all heard the riders at the same moment. They all looked toward the north, as the five Indians rode up on their hunting ponies.

"Oh, no!" Kitta breathed out.

Iron Knife was in their fore, looking very fierce at the moment. They rode right up to within a few yards of the camp, and Iron Knife and the father of the Shoshoni boy scowled at his fallen figure, bound and beaten. They all were armed with bows and tomahawks.

Ranko bent slowly and picked up the empty rifle. But Madame panicked. "I'll get the ammunition!" she cried out. She turned and ran to the nearest wagon.

The Shoshoni boy's father drew an arrow from its quiver, set it on the bowstring, pulled the bow back, and released the arrow. It caught Madame in the middle of her back, just before she turned a corner to get out of their range.

She grabbed at her back as she fell. But the arrow had pierced her heart. She quivered on the ground, and was dead.

Ranko was livid. *"You damn savages!"* he yelled at them in Romany. He lifted the rifle, forgetting it was not loaded, and aimed it at Iron Knife, who had come on into the camp. Iron knife drew a tomahawk from a sheath, and threw it quickly at Ranko. It buried itself in his chest.

Ranko's aged eyes grew very large, and then he

was hitting the ground on his back, both hands now clutching desperately at the axe, where it had made a fist-size hole in his chest. He gasped out a ragged sound, and died there.

"Oh, Holy Spirit!" Kitta muttered.

Vali was scared now. He turned and tried to run, but a mounted rider stopped him, knocking him down.

In a moment, the Shoshonis were dismounting and looking Ranko and Madame over. Kitta and her son stood among them, saying nothing. The Shoshoni boy's father untied him, and the boy smiled at Vali.

A Shoshoni brave led the horses out of the compound, and Iron Knife came over and yanked his tomahawk out of Ranko's chest. He wiped blood from it onto Ranko's trousers, and then looked toward Kitta.

"Gypsies," he said in English. He spat on the ground at her feet.

"Please," Kitta replied in English. "Don't kill my son and me. I didn't want them to harm the boy."

Vali came up to Iron Knife. "You leave us alone! When my grandfather gets here—"

Iron Knife backhanded the boy hard, knocking him to the ground.

Vali lay there wide-eyed, breathing hard, tears welling in his dull eyes. Suddenly he looked very scared.

Iron Knife cast a contemptuous look at him,

then turned back to Kitta. "You are the ones who had McComb's woman."

Kitta lowered her gaze in fear. "It was Skinner who killed her. Not us."

"Where are the others?" Iron Knife said. "How far behind?" He glanced out toward the horizon.

Kitta thought quickly. "Not far," she said.

Iron Knife looked into her eyes, and then smiled. "You are a liar. Like all Gypsies."

"Please," she said quietly.

"All Gypsies are vermin," Iron Knife added.

Kitta closed her eyes. "Oh, Mighty Del," she whispered, exhorting her Gypsy god. "Save us from these savages, my son and me."

Iron Knife did not understand the Romany. He came close to Kitta now, looking her over. Vali rose from the ground, and ran to her, crying. "They're going to kill us! They're going to kill us!"

Iron Knife got an angry look on his face, and slapped Vali down again. This time Vali hit the ground harder, and blood appeared at his mouth. Iron Knife went and kicked the boy in the side, and Vali yelled pitifully.

"Keep out of the way! And be silent!" Iron Knife yelled back.

Vali saw the hard look in Iron Knife's eyes, and quit making all the noise. He lay there awkwardly, holding his face and sobbing almost inaudibly.

Iron Knife turned back to Kitta, and came very close to her. He ran his hand through her long, dark hair. She drew back, but made no protest.

The other Indians came close around her, and she was terrified. Iron Knife put a hand on her breast, and felt the full curve of it. Kitta flinched, and gasped slightly.

"She has beauty," he said in Shoshoni to the others.

"Unclothe her," another Indian said.

"Let the boy watch how men make use of a woman," another said, laughing.

"We will all punish her between her legs," another said. "Then Iron Knife may have her scalp. Look at the hair."

Iron Knife stepped back a step, took his bow, and caught the end of it on the hem of Kitta's long dress. He lifted the dress slowly up Kitta's thighs, as she stood there rigid, breathing hard. Finally he got the hem up to where they could all see Kitta's private places. She had no underclothing on. Iron Knife and the others stared for a moment at the dark place between her thighs, then Iron Knife let the dress drop back to her ankles.

"Yes, we will all take her," a Shoshoni said, a broad-chested, muscular one with a scar across his left eye. He was excited by the brief view of Kitta. "Someone hold the boy."

He came up and grabbed at Kitta's dress, and ripped at the neckline, and part of it came away. Kitta jumped and let out a small cry, and her left breast was exposed. She stumbled backward and a second Shoshoni grabbed her. She struggled in his grasp for a moment, and her exposed flesh excited them even more. But then came Iron Knife's sharp command.

"No, wait!" he said.

The other Shoshoni stared at him, the one who held Kitta.

"Release her," Iron Knife said.

The fellow looked at him quizzically, but followed orders. Kitta stumbled away from him, trying to hide her breast. Vali, on the ground, was crying more audibly again.

"What is it?" the brawny Shoshoni beside Iron Knife said.

"I think I will keep this one," Iron Knife said. "You know I have not taken a woman yet. I will take this Gypsy to my tipi."

"She belongs to all of us!" the broad one protested. "We will all use her, right now. Then we will amuse ourselves in killing her!"

"She is a Gypsy!" the one said who had been holding her. "A child killer! A slave trader! You saw what they were doing to this boy of ours, when we came up!"

Iron Knife turned to him angrily. "I am Iron Knife!" he said in a loud, booming voice. "Do you doubt my authority in this?"

A silence fell over the others. They eyed him with surly looks. "Silver Wolf has exclaimed at my restraint in claiming spoils of our victories over our traditional enemies. Well, I now claim this woman as mine. She will be my slave. The boy I give to the family of this abused Shoshoni youth."

The brawny Shoshoni muttered a Shoshoni obscenity, and turned darkly and walked to their mounts. The others then relaxed about it, and began leaving. One of them, the one who had held Kitta, yanked Vali to his feet, and spoke harshly into Vali's face. "Do not think this is good fortune, son of a coyote! You will learn what it is like to be owned by the People!"

Vali had no idea what the man was talking about. He was just glad to be alive. He made no attempt to resist as the Indian dragged him off to a mount.

Iron Knife took hold of Kitta's long hair, and pulled her head back slightly with it, so that her gaze met his. He was very close to her, his face in hers.

"You are claimed as my woman," he said to her in English. "Do you understand?"

Kitta nodded tensely. She saw the other Shoshoni lift Vali up onto a mount. "Yes."

"If you behave, you will live," Iron Knife went on. "If you do not, I cannot guarantee your future. Or that of your son."

She looked into those hard but rather handsome eyes. "I understand." She glanced at Madame's and Ranko's bodies, and shuddered slightly.

"Forget them," Iron Knife said. "Forget you are a Gypsy. You will never see another one."

Kitta looked at him.

"From this time on, for as long as it lasts for you, you are Shoshoni."

Kitta felt a heavy weight inside her, trying to drag her down to the ground. But she would not let it. She would try to survive. For herself, and for her son.

A moment later, Iron Knife swung her aboard his stallion. The other Indians were now finished with looting the two wagons, carrying away with them clothing and food. Now one of them was setting fire to them. The flames crackled and rose, and black smoke curled skyward. The Indian with Vali had already started off toward Silver Wolf's village.

As Kitta rode off behind Iron Knife on his mount, she took one last look at the terrible scene they were leaving.

Madame had had a dark vision about the outcome of this trip to the Far West, in her crystal ball. She had told only Kitta.

Now that vision was a reality.

Chapter Twelve

When Lazlo had seen the buzzards come circling in over Camargue's corpse, he had gone out and buried the body in a shallow grave. Just so he would not have to look at it. He had never really liked Camargue, and he felt no grief now. But the corpse reminded him that McComb was here, and that he was deadly. He also threw the corpse of Atwood in with Camargue.

Unlike Skinner, who had always ravaged and killed rather recklessly, without concern for his own safety, Lazlo was a somewhat careful man. He weighed the odds, and calculated the risks to himself. It was the Gypsy in him. Now, on this late afternoon at the Camargue campsite, after he had piled the Atwood corpse into the same grave with that of Camargue, he sat and worried about McComb. If it had been him there alone, he would probably have run. The fact was, he had had a chance to get a good look at McComb when the mountain man was in that cage during his captivity with them, and he had been afraid of him, even with McComb behind bars. When that half savage would hurl a dark look at Lazlo from that cage, little tremors of dark terror would prickle through his spine like icicles down the back of his shirt. The feeling McComb gave you, when he sent you that hate-filled look, Lazlo decided, was like the terror a man on foot feels when he rounds a curve in a trail and meets a snarling grizzly ten feet away. Except that somehow it was even more terrifying with McComb. There was a rational dedication to violence written across McComb's face that filled you with black uncertainty about your future, and haunted you long after the confrontation was past, making your breath come short and your sleep sweat-stained.

Skinner stepped down out of the nearby Gypsy wagon, and stared out over the plain, to the horizon. Lazlo followed his gaze, and saw that the sun was just touching the horizon out there. Between them and that reddish orb, a half-dozen antelope loped across the high buffalo grass.

"He ain't coming," Skinner said.

Lazlo eyed him balefully.

"We're going to have to go after him." Skinner came over and stood near Lazlo. He had taken his shirt off, and he was all thick muscle and meat. His belly stuck out some over his belt. He pulled his shirt off a low stump and shrugged it on. He stood there buttoning it, looking morose.

"We'll go some time after dark."

"If he's expecting us," Lazlo said, "he'll be dangerous, Mule."

Skinner looked at him. "You ain't thinking of weaseling out of this on me, are you?"

Lazlo held his gaze. "You know better than that, Mule."

"Do I?"

"I'm just saying, we got to be careful. We're riding into his gun."

Skinner looked out toward the greenhorn camp. "Well, he ain't no goddamn Daniel Boone," he said. "He's just a trapper, he probably don't even know how to use no sidearm. He got awful lucky, when he took me in before. He's just your ordinary mountain man."

Lazlo grunted. "I never saw nothing ordinary about him," he ventured.

Skinner regarded Lazlo narrowly, tucking the shirt in now. "I admit he's more animal than man. And he's trail-smart as a goddamn Comanche. But let me tell you something, Lazlo. I don't mind that a bit. I killed me a Kodiak once, did I ever tell you that? Weighed damn near two thousand pounds. I stood my ground with that brute towering over my head, and put a dozen shots into him. I was gored and trampled by a goddamn buffalo, and ended up cutting its heart out. You think I can't handle some goddamn cave-man type? I thought you had some guts, Lazlo."

"McComb is no bear," Lazlo said. "And he's no buffalo. But I told you I'm with you. Now lay off me, Mule."

Skinner grinned. "Well. The boy has got some sand, after all. Pleased to see it, Lazlo."

"Hell," Lazlo said, rising and looking off toward the other camp. His right hand went unconsciously to the gun on his hip, and rested on it.

"You know what we're going to do?" Skinner said, coming up beside him. "We're going to take that bastard alive."

Lazlo looked at him.

"We're going to make sure we don't hit him in any vital parts," he continued. "Then, when we got him, we'll tie the son of a bitch up."

"What for?" Lazlo said, remembering the last time he had been talked out of killing McComb immediately. Now the man who had made him stop was dead. Killed by McComb.

"Because I want him to go slow," Skinner said with that evil grin. He looked past Lazlo. "We'll build a nice fire, maybe. And erect us a spit over the fire, a big, sturdy one. We'll hog-tie the trapper hand and foot to that spit, about three feet above the fire, stripped buck naked. Then we'll roast him to a nice brown. Slowlike. Partway through it, he'll start screaming and hollering,

236

and that will be the best part." He paused, and was envisioning all of it. "Of course, we won't pay no attention. After a while, the hollering will stop, and we'll just go on cooking his hide."

Lazlo stared hard at him.

"Won't that be kind of nice?" Skinner said to him.

Lazlo knew now that Skinner was even crazier than when he had gone off to prison. "Sure, Mule," he said glumly.

Skinner had just begun to remark further on what they would do to McComb, once they had subdued him, when he stopped and stared again out away from camp. Lazlo did, too.

There was a rider out there.

"It's him!" Lazlo said breathlessly. "He decided to come for us!"

Skinner glanced at him disgustedly. "That ain't him, for Christ's sake."

Skinner was right. The rider was a slight man, making a thin silhouette as he rode toward them. As he came closer, Skinner saw that the fellow was wearing rimless spectacles under a narrow hat brim, and then he could see the lean, bony features, and the stringy, long hair.

"What the hell," he said.

"What?" Lazlo said.

"I'll be a son of a bitch," Skinner said.

"Who is it?" Lazlo said.

Skinner ignored him. The rider came right on

237

up to the camp, and stopped just thirty yards away. He stared hard at Skinner.

"Skinner?" he said loudly.

Skinner shook his head sidewise. "Wylie," he said.

It was the man he had shared the cell with, at Devil's Hole. He had thought he would never see the man's face again.

Wylie rode on up to them. He stared at Skinner some more. "I'll be damned," he said in his thin voice. He glanced at Lazlo for a moment. "Skinner."

"How the hell did you get out, Wylie?" Skinner said.

Wylie looked as sallow as ever, and undernourished. But Skinner knew he had killed a couple of men, that the law did not know about. Wylie had been at Devil's Hole for cattle rustling. Wylie dismounted now. He was wearing eastern-style clothing, and looked like a grocery clerk out on a weekend ride.

"The place was getting crowded." Wylie grinned, coming over to them. "They had to let some of us out early. The warden considered me a model prisoner." The grin widened. He looked over at Lazlo again. "Is this your Gypsy friend?"

Skinner grunted. "Yeah. Yuray Lazlo. Lazlo, this is the dung-heap I had to bunk with at the prison."

Lazlo nodded, and proffered his hand, and

238

Wylie shook it. Lazlo thought Wylie looked rat-faced.

"Mighty pleasured," Wylie said flatly.

"What are you doing way out in this direction?" Skinner asked him.

"Going west," Wylie said. "Thought I might make my fortune in California. How far is the next settlement?"

"Hell, there ain't no settlements ahead of you," Skinner told him. "There's just Indians. Can you talk Indian, Wylie?"

Wylie sighed. "Not much," he said.

"You're going to need a lot of luck then," Skinner said. "All by yourself out here."

Wylie nodded his agreement. "Did you ever find that trapper, Mule? The one you called McComb?"

Now Skinner grinned. He turned to Lazlo. "Did I find him, Lazlo?"

"He found us," Lazlo said. The grin slid off Skinner's face.

"Oh. It's that way," Wylie commented, watching Skinner's meaty face. He knew even better than Lazlo that you don't do anything to add to Skinner's naturally ornery disposition.

Skinner dropped a brittle look on Lazlo. "Okay. He found us. But we got him just the same, ain't we?"

"Yeah, Mule," Lazlo said disconsolately. "We got him."

Skinner jerked a thumb over his shoulder. "He's out there, Wylie. Just over the horizon. At a wagon train camp. We was just getting ready to go kill him."

Wylie frowned slightly. "He's with a wagon train?"

Skinner shook his head, grinning. "You tell him, Lazlo."

Lazlo explained it all to him, in short, flat monotone. He had little interest in killing McComb now. Especially he did not like the idea of playing cat and mouse with the likes of the mountain man. It was dangerous. He wished he were with Madame and Kitta, not realizing what had happened to them.

"So you see, you arrived at a real good time, my boy," Skinner was saying to Wylie.

Wylie looked at him. "How do you mean, Mule?"

Skinner clapped a heavy hand on Wylie's shoulder, jarring him. Wylie adjusted the spectacles on his nose. "Why, you can have the pleasure of helping us kill McComb." Skinner grinned.

Wylie's face went slack. He spoke carefully. "Mule, you know I ain't got no interest in that trapper. I ain't even good with guns. No, I think I'll pass on that."

Skinner held Wylie's gaze, and Wylie got a memory flash of Skinner biting the head off that rat, in their cell that gloomy night. The last thing he wanted to do was rile Skinner. But Skinner now had another grin on his beefy face.

"Maybe I can change your mind," Skinner said. He went to the wagon and got a saddlebag with most of the loot from the wagon train in it. He brought it over to them, and reached into it and pulled out several gold coins. He took Wylie's hand and slapped them into it.

"Now what do you think?" Skinner said.

"Mule —" Lazlo said darkly.

"Shut up!" Skinner told him in a suddenly harsh voice.

Wylie looked from the handful of gold to Lazlo, and then to Skinner. "You want me to have this, to ride over there with you?"

"Three guns will make it more certain that we can take him alive," Skinner said.

Wylie regarded him curiously. "I thought you wanted to kill him."

"Oh, I do," Skinner said. "But carefully."

Wylie glanced at Lazlo, and caught his eye, and saw the meaningful look there. He looked back down at the gold. It was just what he needed to get him where he wanted to go.

Finally, Wylie responded. "Okay. I'll help you with him. If I ain't getting crossways of nobody here." He met Lazlo's gaze again.

"Hell, Lazlo don't mind about me paying you something. Ain't that right, Lazlo?"

Lazlo hesitated. Actually, since he was involved in this, it wasn't a bad development to have one more gun. They could get plenty of gold later.

"Right, Mule," he said.

"You see, Wylie? You got yourself some easy money. Hell, after we have our fun with McComb, we'll probably ride out, too. You can go with us if you want to. I'll show you how to get a lot more of that yellow stuff." He grinned broadly, and it looked unnatural on him.

Wylie grinned back, less widely. "You got a deal, Mule." He stuffed the coins into a pouch. "You got a gun for me?"

"There's a couple rifles in the wagon," Skinner said. "And plenty of ammo." He looked into a darkening sky. "I thought we'd go about midnight. But maybe we'll wait till just before dawn. There might be more chance of catching him asleep. Either of you have a problem with that?"

Lazlo shook his head sidewise, and Wylie added, "Sounds fine to me, Mule."

"If we do it right, he won't know what hit him," Skinner told them, staring out over the almost-black landscape. "We'll go in like goddamn Indians. And remember, I want him alive. If you have to shoot him, don't kill him. I don't want no bullet in his brain. That would be too nice for him."

"Mule," Lazlo said. "Are you sure we

242

shouldn't just put this wild man down any way we can? Just remembering him in that cage makes my flesh crawl."

Skinner regarded him with disgust. "Just do it like I tell you, Gypsy. You'll be all right."

Wylie looked from Skinner to Lazlo, and saw the fear in Lazlo's face, and hoped Skinner was right.

The next sunup would tell the tale.

Over at the greenhorn campsite, McComb worked on into the darkness to prepare for the assault he knew was coming. He had brought a dozen cartridges for the Sharps buffalo rifle with him, and he now loaded that long gun as well as the shotgun. He took the tripod for it out of a saddle scabbard, and set it up on the perimeter of the camp, nearest the Gypsy encampment. With the traps set, and the knives in place in the ground, Apache-style, McComb was ready.

He did not get too comfortable. He took a chair out of the nearest wagon, and set it right in the middle of camp, a hard, straight chair, and sat down on it. The shotgun lay across his lap, and the revolver hung on his hip. He did not build a fire. He got a stogie cigar out and smoked it slowly, enjoying it. It got to be mid-evening. He drank a few swigs of some cheap, rot-gut whiskey he had found in a wagon. It went down like lemonade to McComb. The hardest liquor did not make him drunk, a phenomenon the Apaches had never understood. He waited, and he waited some more.

At midnight, he figured Skinner was not coming for a while. He'll come in the wee hours, he thought. Skinner had, in the past, pulled off some robberies just before dawn.

McComb took his hat off and threw it onto the ground, then rubbed a muscular hand through his thick, dark beard. He could not be groggy from fatigue when they came, Skinner and Lazlo. He remembered the shallow grave he had buried the bodies in, and how he had put Jameson on the outer edge of it. He left the chair, went out to the grave site, and dug up Jameson. He dragged the corpse into camp again, and set the body upright on the chair he had been sitting on. He placed the Sharps rifle in Jameson's hands, resting it across the corpse's knees. He tied Jameson to the chair, so the body would not fall off.

Another Apache trick.

McComb went and crawled under a wagon, on the far side of camp from the Gypsy campsite. In high weeds. He curled up there with the shotgun, and he napped.

A rustling of grass, and he was awake. It was a rabbit scurrying to a hole. Later, a coyote let out a long wail, out on the plain, and he was awake again.

He was dreaming, when the shot came. He was back in his South Pass cabin with Nalin, and she had just undressed and was inviting him to bed.

He came awake like an antelope, the rifle shot still echoing in his ears. Raising up in the weeds, he saw that the Jameson corpse had been knocked sidewise by hot lead.

He squinted into the darkness. A clock in his head told him that it was not long before dawn. There was just a hint of light in the eastern sky, but the plain was very dark.

McComb lay there, watching and listening. Skinner had arrived, he knew. And at this moment, he probably thought McComb was hit.

Actually, it had been Lazlo who had fired at the figure on the chair. He and Wylie were approaching the camp from its near side to them, and Skinner had gone around the back side of the site. Lazlo had seen the seated corpse first, and thought he saw it move. He had panicked and fired, out beyond McComb's traps. He had fired low, following Skinner's instructions, hoping to hit the figure in the hip or leg, but the rifle had shot high and smacked the corpse in the low chest.

Back in the high grass on the far side, Skinner had sworn under his breath, and hoped Mc-

Comb was not dead. He stared hard at the figure on the chair, and swore aloud. He had to give his position away.

"Keep down! That ain't him!" he yelled out.

McComb, still under the wagon, turned quickly. Skinner's voice had come from behind him.

They've surrounded the camp, he thought.

McComb had the night vision of a wolf, and he could enhance it by moving his head about, as he had seen cougars do. He had already spotted the heads of Wylie and Lazlo out there, and was surprised when Skinner's voice had come from a different direction. He knew now that Skinner had found a third man to join him in the assault.

They were all out there about a hundred yards, just outside his hidden devices. McComb crawled out from under the wagon, on his belly, dragging the shotgun with him. He went as silent as a panther. He crawled toward Wylie and Lazlo, and away from Skinner, skirting the center of the compound. A half-moon shone brightly overhead, and the corpse of Jameson looked eerie sitting there on that straight chair, like a demon risen from Hades, waiting to take its revenge on its murderers.

Wylie had not understood Skinner's message. He thought that Skinner surely did not see what he and Lazlo did—that slumped figure on the

246

chair, shot by Lazlo. Wylie rose, and walked slowly in toward the camp.

In camp, McComb waited. He had placed the traps close enough that he could defend himself with the shotgun. He got onto his knee, beside a wagon. In that same moment, Wylie came in too close, and stepped into a beaver trap.

Wylie felt the cold steel smash into his ankle above his shoe, and he rose from his crouch like a jack-in-the-box, yelling loudly.

McComb raised the shotgun toward the flailing figure of Wylie, and squeezed off a round. The night was filled with the booming of a yellow explosion, and Wylie was hit by lead in the face, the chest, the neck. His yelling was cut off abruptly, and he went flying backward, taking the trap with him.

There was some muffled croaking in the grass then, and some kicking of the legs, and Wylie died there with his dreams of riches in California.

Lazlo, only thirty yards away, stared in raw fear toward the dead Wylie, then both he and Skinner were firing at the place where the shotgun had exploded in the night.

But McComb was no longer there. He had rolled quickly to his left, then crawled to the other end of the wagon that hid him. Bullets from Lazlo's rifle and Skinner's Derringer revolver dug up dirt where McComb had crouched, but came nowhere close to him.

"Shit," Lazlo muttered to himself. Then he yelled to Skinner, knowingly giving his location away. *"He's got traps out here!"*

"I know that, goddamn it!" Skinner yelled back. McComb noted that the voice came from a slightly different position.

The adrenaline was pumping into Skinner. He kept low, but he was nerved up to the point of frenzy. He knew Wylie was dead. *"That was it, McComb!"* he yelled out in the gravel voice. *"You better enjoy that, it's the last trouble you're ever going to cause me, you son of a bitch! You're mine, McComb! You're going slow, you bastard! Real slow!"*

"Shut up, Mule!" Lazlo yelled out nervously.

Skinner laughed loudly, insanely. *"You think I'm afraid to warn this motherless beast what's in store for him? Not me, Gypsy! Not his executioner, by God!"*

McComb peered into the lightening darkness toward the voice, trying to find Skinner, but Skinner was keeping well down. McComb was cool, emotionless. Even in this situation, he did not think of himself as the hunted. He was the hunter, they were his prey. As for replying to Skinner, it did not even occur to him. He was not here to banter with these men, to prove anything verbally to them. He was there to kill them.

Lazlo wanted to get this over with, now. He

248

was terrified of not leaving this place alive. He did not care if he killed McComb with one shot, he just wanted to kill him. And Skinner would just have to live with that. He rose in a crouch, and moved forward.

And stepped directly on one of McComb's hidden knives.

The sharp point and blade sliced right through Lazlo's thin-soled shoe, into his flesh and his weight drove the point on through the top of his foot.

He did not yell as loudly as Wylie had, but a loud hissing sound issued from his throat, and he straightened, then went down.

In that instant when he rose to his full height, McComb detached himself from the side of the wagon, leaning away from it, and his finger whitened over the trigger of the shotgun, to fire its second load. But Lazlo went down so fast, he had no chance to fire. Then, while he was exposed to Skinner for that split-second, Skinner spotted him clearly in the lightening sky, and he fired the Derringer and hit McComb squarely in the back.

McComb felt the hot lead penetrate his flesh, just under the floating ribs, and to the left of his spine. It traveled through him like a hot poker, knocking him against the wagon violently, and throwing him to the ground.

"I got him! I got the son of a bitch!" Skinner

was yelling wildly. *"I hope you ain't dead, god-damn you, McComb!"*

Lazlo, lying on the ground out there trying to figure out what had happened to him, heard the news with restrained satisfaction. He saw the knife point coming out of his foot, and realized it had gone right through. He grabbed at the handle of it, beneath his foot, and pulled the weapon out. He hissed again in nausea and pain, and his shoe began filling with blood.

"Oh, God," he gritted out. He just lay there, breathing hard. He was not going to try to go on in, he would let Skinner kill McComb now. Any way that suited him.

McComb turned onto his back, and felt the place under his ribs where the bullet had exited in the front of his torso. It had hit him cleanly, closer to his side than his spine, and he figured it had hit nothing vital. He put his hand to the exit wound, and there was a lot of wet there. Pain and shock washed through him in waves, and he thought for a moment he might pass out. A lesser man would have been out like a light, but McComb was no ordinary man.

He still had hold of the shotgun, the gun slightly hidden by the wagon he had fallen beside. He lay there, waiting for Skinner. He could not see where he was, but he heard him now, coming through the grass. He saw a scrap of cloth underneath the wagon, something of the women who had been killed. He brought it to him, and stuffed it into the wound in his side. He grunted with renewed pain, and blackness welled in again for a moment, but he knew now that the shot would not kill him.

The sound of Skinner's coming got louder. The sun was edging above the horizon now, and light was slowly filling the sky. McComb could see big boots walking toward him, from the other side of the wagon. Then, Skinner was there.

He looked big and ugly when he rounded the corner of the wagon and looked down on Mc-Comb, the Derringer out in front of him. His eyes looked wild, and his breath was coming labored.

"Well, well," Skinner grunted out in deep satisfaction. "Now, ain't this nice." He could not see the shotgun yet, the gun McComb still held in his right fist, his finger on that second trigger.

Skinner stopped a few feet away. "You ain't got no idea how much I been looking forward to this," he said, the Derringer aimed at McComb's face. "All through them lice-infested days at that hellhole of a prison, McComb. All through them long nights, smelling other people's piss and looking at them gray walls. I thought of this, McComb. What I would do to you, when this time come."

McComb did not reply. He held his hand over

the hole in him, to keep the cloth in the wound. His deep blue eyes burned a look into Skinner that would have made some men urinate in their trousers. But he said nothing. He had not come here for talking.

"I'm glad to see you ain't hit bad, mountain man." Skinner grinned. He was only fifteen feet away. "I got time to make your passing real nice for you. What would you prefer? Roasting over a campfire to a golden brown? Skinning out, inch by inch, like the Blackfeet and Bannocks do? Or maybe you'd prefer I just get over you and just kick you to death, leaving your head for last?"

McComb prepared himself. His right fist gripped the shotgun. He could not wait too long, or Skinner would move in and see the gun under the wagon.

"Well, since you ain't got no preference, maybe I'll just roast you on a low fire," Skinner said, grinning more widely. "Soon as I can get that dumb Gypsy in here to tie you up. *Hey, Lazlo, get your ass in here!*"

Skinner looked away from McComb for just a second, and lowered the muzzle of the Derringer slightly. In that moment, McComb slid the shotgun out from under the wagon, raised the business end, and fired off its second round.

Skinner saw the movement at the last second, and raised the Derringer to fire. It did fire, too, but a split second after the shotgun. The shotgun blast hit Skinner in the groin and right thigh, and blew his leg completely off. Skinner was picked up off the other leg, a look of abject surprise on his meaty face, and was thrown to the ground violently. The shot from the Derringer kicked up dirt beside McComb's head, but did not hit him.

McComb dropped the shotgun heavily to the ground, breathing hard. Skinner lay twenty feet away, in the peach-hued light of the new sun, staring wide-eyed toward the sky, trying to understand what had happened, and how events had turned around so dramatically, and so quickly.

McComb got up onto his knee, and felt a sickness inside him. But he knew now he would be all right. He pulled the Bowie knife from its sheath on his belt, and crawled over to Skinner. He came up beside Skinner, and Skinner looked up at him. He was going into shock.

"Don't — kill me," he grated out.

Out in the high grass, Lazlo's voice came to them. *"Skinner! What happened? Are you okay?"*

McComb stuck the point of the big knife up under Skinner's chin. "You ought to stayed in Texas, bear shit," he growled out in a voice Skinner wished he had never heard. Then he drove the blade up into Skinner's skull.

Skinner jumped upward as if he were getting up to leave, and his ugly eyes saucered, and then his limbs were jerking about spasmodically. In a moment, he fell back and was still.

"Skinner?" From Lazlo, again.

McComb turned toward the sound. The Gypsy, the one who had given Nalin a life of hell, a fate worse than her eventual death at the hands of Skinner.

McComb rose to his feet, and was very dizzy. He had left the knife in Skinner's skull, he never wanted to see it again. Now he drew the Patterson-Colt revolver, and turned and began walking toward Lazlo.

The sun was finally up, and it was easy to spot Lazlo. McComb came right up to him where he lay in the high grass. Lazlo had his Tranter sidearm out, and was aiming it right at McComb's chest. McComb saw it, but came on up to him, with that look in his eyes that bled Lazlo white under it. Lazlo was more terrified than he had ever been in his life. When McComb got to within a dozen feet, he lost control of his bowels and soiled his trousers. Then he hurled the gun away.

"Oh, God! Don't kill me!" he blurted out. *"It was Skinner who killed the Apache woman, not me. I tried to save her."*

McComb came and stood over Lazlo, the revolver hanging loosely in his right hand. Lazlo felt as if a grizzly was standing over him, intent on ripping him to shreds. The stink of him came up to McComb, and McComb shook his head sidewise, slowly.

"You know you got to die, I guess."

Utter panic filled Lazlo's face. "I tell you, it was Skinner! Honest to God! Hey, I've got gold you can have! At the Gypsy wagons. Skinner took it from these people. I didn't have any part in it. Take it, it's yours!"

"You're snail slime, Lazlo," McComb said, in a flat, tired voice. The dizziness came back. He raised the gun, and casually blew a hole in Lazlo's face, just under the left eye. Lazlo hit the ground violently with his right arm, and was dead. There was a lot of bone and gray matter scattered through the grass.

"Hell," McComb said to himself. "I ruined the scalp."

He stood there for a moment, getting some strength into him. The sun was rising on a clear, warm day. He took one last look at Lazlo, then turned and walked across the plain to where his stallion was still picketed to a small mesquite tree. The animal had bucked and whinnied during the shooting, but now was calmer.

McComb led it past the campsite, got his long guns that he needed for his hunting, and boarded the mount. Blowflies were already gathering on Skinner. McComb liked the sound of their low buzzing.

He spurred the pinto, and rode off toward Silver Wolf's village, where he would be tended, and heal.

Then he would head back to South Pass, where the beavers were thick as bankers in hell.

It was a return worth looking forward to.